The Woman on the Knoll

Duncan King

The Woman on the Knoll © 2014

by Duncan King.

ISBN 978-1466430990

All rights reserved. No part of this book may be reproduced, scanned or distributed in any printed or electronic form without written permission.

Printed in the United States of America

This is a work of fiction. Names, characters, places and incidents either are the product of the author's imagination or are used fictitiously and any resemblance to actual persons, living or dead, business establishments, companies, events or locales is entirely coincidental.

Nosmog Press
2014

For information:

Nosmog Press
PO Box 235
Lee Vining, CA93541
nosmog@yahoo.com

For Ellen, who always helps

Thanks also to Terry, Ailsa, Jessica, Steven and Sammy for being there, and to Dave Carle and Jim Watkins for their inputs. Special thanks to Ellen for multiple readings, suggestions, and edits. Needless to say all errors belong to the author.

During 1963 there were three attempts on the life
of President John F. Kennedy

Two were not successful

The Woman on the Knoll

First

The president's aide stuck his head into the communications bay.

"Any news?"

No response. He leaned in further and saw the radio operator hunched over the console, headphones tight over his ears. He tapped the airman on the shoulder and got an irritated wave from one hand as the other frantically scribbled on a message pad.

He waited, the cigarette burning down between his fingers. The muffled air stream seemed louder as he stood there and watched the spiraling smoke get sucked into the overhead vent.

"What?"

He looked back down and saw the radioman looking up at him, one headphone pulled away from an ear.

"Any news?"

"Nothing interesting," the radio operator said.

"Why? You expecting something?"

The fresh faced young man in the short sleeved shirt and tie blinked behind his wire rimmed glasses. "No, not really, but the president told me to keep checking in with you."

The operator restrained himself from blinking back and asking when high school kids got to be on staff.

"Your first time?"

"On Air Force One? Yeah."

"Well I'll tell you. When something comes in that the president needs to hear about, you'll be the first to know, okay?" He started to turn back toward his console.

The aide leaned against the doorway and adjusted his tie clip with one hand while fiddling with his cigarette with the other.

"Okay. So how long till we land?"

The kid sounded like he was from New England.

"Depends."

Didn't he know that some folks had real jobs?

"On what?"

"On how long a piece of string is."

"What?"

"Listen, kid. I don't fly this sucker. You got a question about the telex, the phones or the radio, you come ask me. You want to learn how to fly then go ask the pilot."

He pulled his headphone back down, turned away from the doorway, and tinkered with the radio controls.

"And don't slouch against the bulkhead. You make this expensive airframe look untidy."

The aide straightened up. "Hey Sarge, I didn't mean anything by it, I just…"

The radio operator swiveled back toward him.

The Woman on the Knoll

"Look kid, I just finished patching the First Lady through to her father and I've got the Secretary of State on hold for the president. After that I have to send a message to the US ambassador in Paris and then decode an update from NORAD. And don't call me Sarge, my name's Jim. If you want to be useful go get me some fresh coffee. If you don't want to be useful then just go."

The doorway was suddenly clear.

The radio operator chuckled.

"At least Jack's flunkies were born this century, not like Ike's."

He leaned back and luxuriated in the modern communications bay. It was a damn sight better than in the previous loaner planes from the Air Force, and Jackie had done a great design job on the outside. The papers and TV loved the style and they got huge press coverage now wherever they visited. They'd wowed Europe even before Jack's comment about being the guy 'who accompanied Jackie to Paris' and the 'Ich bin ein Berliner' speech. If only there was room for one more person at the radios life would be perfect.

A mug of coffee appeared on the console beside him, steaming and fresh smelling. He only noticed the faintest ripple on its surface, nothing like the angry sloshing he'd been used to on the old propeller transports. The new RC125, the president's customized version of the Boeing 707, was as smooth as silk.

He looked up and noticed the kid was back, looking nervous.

"Did you need cream or sugar, Jim?"

Definitely a Massachusetts accent.

"No thanks." He sipped the brew then nodded his

appreciation. "Is this from his stash?"

The kid smiled then offered his hand. "My name's Jim too," he said.

"That's confusing… one of us will have to go." The radio operator laughed at the aide's startled reaction and waved his arms in negation. "No. It's okay…I was only joking."

"Are you too busy to talk?"

"No, it's quieter now." The kid seemed eager to please and with Jim less in his face the accent was coming through as pure Boston now.

"Is it always this warm in here?"

"When we replace these radios with those new hardened transistor types then we'll be able to cool it down more, but for now it's nice and cozy. Even Jackie came in here one time when the air conditioning was stuck on…"

He felt the plane level out and even through the headphones heard the reduced roar of the four Pratt and Whitney turbofans. At the same time a new voice came over the air. He frowned and started scribbling down the words, unconsciously forming the cursive script as neatly as he could.

The tests he'd taken before being certified for Air Force One were the strictest that he had ever taken and the clarity of his writing under stress had been pushed to the limit. He and two other finalists had even been taken to NASA and strapped into one of their astronaut vomit inducing training machines. Whirling around upside down and almost inside out he still didn't know how he'd managed to transcribe garbled messages legibly. He almost wished now that he'd failed and was back on B-52's flying nuclear standing patrols again. At least those flights had a chance of accomplishing something. On the other hand here he might just witness the President pushing the red button on thousands of warheads, instead of just being on the sharp end of a few.

He suddenly realized that the aide was looking at him strangely and remembered the message. He tore the slip off the pad and handed it to the kid.

"Message from Center. Better make sure the President sees it straightaway."

The kid took the paper and scanned the words. He absorbed the content and disappeared round the bulkhead.

The radio operator leaned back and sipped his coffee.

"For God's sake, Lee, stop fidgeting."

Every time he squirmed in the front passenger seat the butt of his rifle grated on the metal floor of the station wagon. I stopped in mid-tap when I noticed my fingernails were attacking the chrome on the door handle. A gust of wind shook the car as he muttered a reply.

Gray clouds were messing with the sky and the car windows had started to steam up. We were parked on a freeway overpass and every time a vehicle drove by I held my breath, feeling the eyes of its occupants on us. I expected a black and white pull over at any moment. But as Tony had said, this was the best place for a clear shot.

Tony.

I was going to kill him once I got out of this mess. If I did. And preferably slowly.

Johnny was sitting in front of me. He let go of the

steering wheel and glared across at Lee. I leaned back against my seat, wrinkled my nose at the smell of them and tried to breathe through my mouth. They could have showered. It was kind of a special day.

The car wobbled in the wind, out of synch with the rumble of traffic on the freeway below. The butt of the rifle grated on the floor again.

"Lee, cut it out."

He moved his hands and wrapped them tightly round the top of the barrel. I could see where his fingers had left grease marks lower down near the sight. Johnny hunkered down and lit another cigarette.

We waited.

I wondered why the cops hadn't closed off the freeway ramps. Wouldn't that be the obvious thing to do? But the traffic kept flowing.

"Something's wrong," I said.

Silence.

That figured. Lee was too nervous to speak and Johnny couldn't give a rat's ass about what either of us thought. I leaned forward. Johnny's exhaled smoke improved his odor but Lee's sweat smelled even worse close up.

"I said, 'Something's wrong'."

Lee's head swiveled. His breath stank worse than his body but at least he backed me up.

"They're not coming, Johnny. Let's get out of here."

Johnny stared Lee down and then said, "Give them time. They're just running late."

Lee bit on his lower lip. He waved Johnny's cigarette smoke away from his face and cranked his window open. The breeze swirled Marlboro's finest back

The Woman on the Knoll

into my face. I coughed.

"Take it easy, you two." Johnny leaned forward and switched on the radio. The maniacal laughter on the intro to the Surfaris' latest single wailed.

"Sheesh!" he said, and fiddled with the knobs.

We froze as he caught a news flash.

"...and so the president's visit has been canceled. He was en route to Chicago when news came in that Vietnam's President Diem had been assassinated. Air Force One is returning to Washington, so President Kennedy will not attend the Army-Air Force game at Soldier Field today."

"Shit!"

Johnny cranked the engine and we drove off.

Second

The walkie-talkie on the chair between us squawked. I hated the things; either the reception sucked or the batteries died just when you needed them.

Johnny picked it up, listened, and grunted. He looked at me and said, "Twenty-five minutes."

The old wooden floor planks were rough and killing my butt. My back ached from leaning against the hard red brick wall and my leg muscles were tensing up. I stood and stretched, then looked out of the window. We had a perfect view of the street where the motorcade would appear. It would drive directly toward us and then hang a left to run alongside our building. We would never get a better angle for our shots.

"Get back out of sight," Johnny said.

I moved slowly away from the window and looked at him. "You are going to keep your side of the bargain, right?"

Johnny stared back at me. "You just do your part."

"Haven't I so far? It's not my fault Kennedy never showed last time."

He scowled. Normally his face crinkled into the smile that he thought softened the leer on his face. Today

The Woman on the Knoll

his white hair framed narrow eyes and pursed lips.

I frowned back at him. "And where's Lee today?"

"He's covering a different angle." Johnny snickered as though at some inside joke. "You just concentrate on your job."

"I'm surprised you kept him after last time. He gets too nervous and he's a lousy shot."

"Not your problem, but he rated sharpshooter in the marines. He can still be useful, just like you."

Cryptic, but I let it go.

The walkie-talkie crackled again. Johnny grabbed it. His face creased and his body stiffened. After ten seconds he said, "Okay."

He switched off the radio and looked at me. "Grab your gear. We're out of here."

"Why? What's happening?"

"The Tampa cops are increasing security. They're going to check out these buildings."

"How do we know what they're going to do? We have a police spy or something?"

He scowled. "Just get moving. We'll get another chance in Dallas."

Third

It was just a ten minute flight from Carswell AFB to Dallas and the radios were hot all the way. With the pre-flight routines for the pilots, communications checks, updates of security protocols, and standard air safety procedures, hours of prep work went into each flight. If JFK and Jackie had used the limo from the hotel in Fort Worth they'd have got to Dallas just as quickly as flying but it was a more impressive entrance landing at Love Field than driving in on the freeway. Apparently spit and polish counted for votes this fall.

They'd barely left the ground when it was time for the radio operator to secure his coffee mug for landing and the aide leaned over toward him and said, "Any messages?"

Idiot. If there were any message I'd have passed them, to you, wouldn't I?

"No, nothing."

The Secret Service agent standing next to the kid said, "Okay, but stay alert. There's been a lot of concern about this visit."

The two of them disappeared to buckle in for landing.

The Woman on the Knoll

'What else would I do?' the operator thought, as he leaned forward and adjusted the frequency on the radio. Garbled speech came through his headphones and then the wheels hit the ground and they'd arrived at Dallas.

The plane taxied briefly before pausing then the engines spooled down. In the corridor outside the communications bay he heard people gathering at the front doorway. He heard a gentle thump on the fuselage and then the familiar clunk and swish as the door opened. The heat of a fine Texas fall day pushed in through the air-conditioning and the noise of the assembled crowds drifted in with it.

I leaned against the white picket fence and turned the dial on my transistor. When the newscaster's voice came through I reduced the volume and then balanced the radio on the top rail of the fence. Reception sucked as the signal faded in and out.

I looked over the fence and down the sloping grass in front of me to Elm Street. The Dealey Plaza lawn stretched away to Main. To my left it I could see the end of the Texas State Book Depository building and facing it across the street was the DalTex building. After what happened in Tampa I couldn't believe that the cops wouldn't search the buildings overlooking the motorcade route, but Tony had seemed confident. Third time lucky, he'd said, but I wondered. Surely the Secret Service or the FBI would find Lee and Marv in those buildings before the motorcade arrived.

The scratchy radio voice announced, "Air Force

17

One has landed at Love Field and has taxied into position by the red carpet. The aircraft door is opening and the crowd is starting to cheer as the first lady and the president appear at the top of the steps. Jackie is wearing a striking pink suit and a pillbox hat. She just waved and the cheers increased. President Kennedy is smiling. He's waving too, and smoothes down his hair."

I looked around. I was alone up by the fence.

"The wind here is gusting now, but the president has ordered the bubble top removed from the limo so that he can see the crowd better. That means we can see Jackie better too. The Kennedy's aren't Texas' favorite family, but we hear that a quarter million people are lining the parade route. Cynics have said that if the president had come on his own we'd see less than fifty thousand, so I guess most everyone is here to see the first lady.

"The motorcade has now left the airfield and turned onto Turtle Creek. The first large crowds are going wild as they see Jackie. They are pushing forward as the limo approaches and catch the police line unaware. The cops hold their position and the crush eases."

Tony came up from the parking lot behind me and stood at the end of the picket fence by the pergola. He hadn't been involved directly in the first two attempts but this time he wanted no complications. I hardly recognized him in a suit but he looked the part of a Secret Service agent with his normally unruly hair trimmed and tidy. He smirked at me. His last words before I'd set out for the plaza had been, 'You guys have screwed up twice already. This time I'll be there to make sure it goes right.'

He would be waiting for me after this and I hoped I'd live through the next hour to see him. But for now I had

The Woman on the Knoll

to concentrate on the job at hand and hope for a future meeting.

I kept looking for genuine agents but couldn't see any. The motorcade finally rounded the corner onto Elm and headed toward me. I saw a flash of pink and heard the cheers of the crowd getting louder. Some people down there had been waiting for hours; I'd seen them arriving when I'd scouted my position earlier.

Not long to go now. I wondered if I could I see this through.

Most people in Texas, and especially in Dallas, hated Kennedy and his liberalism. The newspapers that morning had decried his landing at Love Field as a sick joke. Spoof wanted posters of him were everywhere. The banner heading Wanted for Treason condemned him as a traitor to the American people. He was accused of betraying the constitution by turning the sovereignty of the US over to the communist controlled United Nations, supporting and encouraging communist inspired racial riots, and illegally invading sovereign US states with federal troops.

There was little separation of state and hate in Dallas that day.

The president's limo crawled along. I couldn't see any Secret Service agents screening his car but there were some hanging onto the sides and rear of the following vehicle. What use were they there? Johnny and Marv would have no problem aiming at this target. Even Lee might not miss.

But where were the agents on the ground? I scanned the mass of people, looking for dark suits, sunglasses, short cropped hairstyles, and hands clutching radios. I couldn't believe there weren't any up here by the fence or on the grass in front of me. Not that I minded. Getting away was always going to be the hardest part. Tony had come up with a good plan, not great, but he, Johnny, and I had a better chance of escaping than Lee and Marv.

The noise below me rose as the people on the grass had their first glimpse of Jackie. I lifted my binoculars and checked out the red brick Texas State Book Depository building where Lee was supposed to be firing from the sixth floor. I couldn't see him but caught a glimpse of Marv on the roof of the DalTex building across the street. He was in a great position for crossfire.

Below me the roaring of the crowd reached a crescendo as the open topped limo cruised forward. I forced myself to relax and loosen my grip on the rifle.

The Woman on the Knoll

Four

I shielded the rifle between my body and the fence and tried to check the surrounding area without looking conspicuous, but the longer I stood there the more self-conscious I felt.

The people waiting on the grass below shuffled closer to the road as the cars drew nearer.

Where was the FBI? They were cutting it close. But maybe they'd already caught Lee.

I checked both ways along the picket fence again but I only saw a baby stroller in the shade of a small tree and Johnny farther along, part concealed by the branches and leaves of the small trees shading the grass and fence.

President Kennedy's limo was now close enough to see the occupants, their heads swiveling as they waved to the crowd. Parents held their babies aloft and flags were waving. I could see older folks who'd been allowed through to the front by southern politeness being pushed forward by the crush. Jackie waved an animated pink arm and JFK smiled as he acknowledged the cheers. Governor Connolly and his wife, sitting in front of the first family, were also waving, but with less extravagant gestures as if to not upstage the real stars of the day. A few of the crowd, mainly Hispanic, booed and held up anti-Cuban signs like 'Bay of Pigs' and 'Fidel must go'.

I raised my rifle and through the scope I could see sweat on the faces of the Secret Service agents, their bodies stiff and awkward as they clung to the limo's side and checked the crowd. One of them looked sick and his face was green as he clutched the car for balance.

Jackie smiled as two babies were lifted to see her, then a pained expression flitted across her face. I remembered her infant son who had died recently. She wiped her eyes and smiled again, probably the last time for weeks.

I checked around. Still nothing suspicious. Along the fence to my right the small tree quivered, although the breeze had now died down. Johnny had disturbed a branch as he raised his carbine.

I sighted on the car and waited. The slight breeze from the car's motion disturbed the president's hair but he patted it in the familiar gesture which Bobby Kennedy would later fashion as his own. I rested my eye from the scope and checked for the final time. No sound yet from the book depository, no alarm signs from the security detail, and no rush of federal agents or police uniforms.

So where was the FBI?

Five seconds.

I rested my rifle in one of the wooden V's on top of the picket fence. My angle of view was rapidly improving.

Two seconds.

The roar became even louder as the nearest crowd section saw the caravan come alongside. I could feel the sun's heat on my back as I leaned forward, moving the sight from Jackie across to the target.

The Woman on the Knoll

One second.

My fiancé's face filled the sights. Would we ever see each other again? I pushed the image away then blinked and focused on the president, my finger taking up the first pressure on the trigger. The first shot came from my left, earlier than I expected and then I fired at almost the same time as Johnny. The recoil hit my shoulder hard. The urban corridors of the buildings made for strange acoustics and the echoes of the shots reverberated round the plaza.

As the faint wisp of smoke wafted away from the barrel I saw a cloud of red through the sight, followed by frantic motion, and a scurrying flash of pink over the back of the seat. A secret service agent jumped from the second car and ran toward the president's. He threw himself on the trunk of the limo and pushed Jackie back into her seat. She then cradled JFK's head in her lap, her pink splotched with his red. Sirens howled as the motorcade slowed, the drivers in shock.

The crowd had been stunned into silence but then a shocked and frightened wailing lifted toward me. One couple was down on the grass with their baby cradled between them. I stared at the scene then shuffled back and down behind the fence.

Why hadn't the FBI shown up?

I heard car engines roar and tires scream as the convoy peeled out.

Now all I had to do was catch up with Tony.

Five

    I held the rifle down by my leg to shield it from view. The shouts and screams coming from the street were getting louder. My brain was screaming 'flee' but I forced myself to walk steadily alongside the fence. I saw that Johnny had already lifted the grating and was climbing down.

    We had practiced the escape twice and developed a smooth routine. Johnny would fire from his position closer to the sewer entrance. His job was to lift the grating, then climb down and grab the flashlight from the ledge where we'd left it. He would then move along a few feet to make room for me. I would follow and close the grating behind me. We would then shuffle a few hundred yards along the tunnel to an exit just by our car in the parking lot. A minute later we were to pick up Lee at the back door of the Texas State Book Depository building and then Marv outside the DalTex building.

    Johnny's rifle was down on the grass and he was shoulder deep in the sewer. I was thirty feet away. I watched as the miserable double crossing bastard picked up his rifle then smiled and winked at me. I'd never liked him. He was treacle smooth, thought he was charming, and

The Woman on the Knoll

claimed to have a lot of success with the ladies. I never understood why. He pulled the sewer grating down with a thunk. That didn't worry me as much as the rattle that followed. I ran over and pulled on the grating but it might have been welded for all the movement I got. He'd wrapped chain around it and padlocked it. I heard his laugh echo in the concrete tube as he shuffled away. The lying bastard had hung me out to dry.

I didn't check around to see if anybody was watching. I already looked suspicious enough. I walked back along the fence hearing the voices on the other side getting louder.

"It was up there."

I heard Tony's voice. "Okay folks, stay clear. There's nothing to see."

"Who says?"

"Secret Service."

I visualized him waving the ID he'd stolen in the nightclub the previous evening.

"Go on back down. Everything's under control."

"But I'm sure I heard firing from behind the fence."

"There were two shots," said a different voice.

"It's all clear up here, folks," Tony said.

I guess that by then he thought he'd given Johnny enough time to get away, because I didn't hear his voice again. Once we were clear the plan had been for Tony to mingle with the crowd and disappear. Obviously he and Johnny had revised the plan, and I wasn't in it.

Six

The stroller was just where I'd left it, under the tree where the baby would be shaded. I walked towards it as confidently as I was able, which wasn't very much as I was holding the rifle down by my side and starting to shake with reaction to the last three minutes. When I reached the stroller I broke down the rifle and stashed the two parts in the red canvas tube that ran from the handle down to the wheels. I arranged the umbrella that was already in the holster so that it covered the rifle parts and we left the shade. As I pushed the stroller toward the pergola the small wheels caught on clumps of grass and jiggled the metal frame. The cotton seat shook and shifted the blanket over the quiet form in the seat. I slowed down and readjusted it.

I walked back past where I'd fired from and heard a small tinny noise. Jeez! Just as well Johnny had abandoned me. In my rush to get away I'd left the transistor radio, covered with my fingerprints, on the fence. I grabbed it and turned it off, then stuffed it under the bedding in the stroller.

I continued on and reached the pergola at the end of the fence. My left shoe caught on the uneven surface and I reminded myself not to walk too quickly. I looked down

The Woman on the Knoll

at the chaos. Below me the couple with the child was still huddled on the grass and a cop was running across the road toward them. Some people were pointing at the TSBD building and some toward the fence where Johnny and I had been standing. Across the road a man holding an opened umbrella closed it, and strode away. On a sunny day? What was that all about?

I looked back to the parking lot and saw Johnny wave as he drove the Nash Rambler station wagon toward the back of the book depository building. Disgusted, I looked away. Down to the right I saw a man in a shabby suit shaking his head. He was standing on a plinth holding a small cine camera. His face was ashen and he was shouting, "They killed him. They killed him. They killed him." The woman standing beside him was quivering.

Some people ran around me to the back of the picket fence.

"I'm sure someone was here."

"Maybe he ran down to the parking lot."

I watched them run toward the parked cars. Then I pushed the stroller down the grass to the sidewalk on Elm. Some huddles of people seemed too shocked to move, others were screaming at the cops about where the shots had come from, and some were still pointing at buildings.

A red-haired woman was in tears, shouting at a cop. "I saw them. Up in those two windows." She was pointing up at the book depository building. "There, on the fifth, no, the sixth floor. See those open windows?"

"No way, lady," another guy said, "I heard shots coming from the roof of that other building on the corner."

In the middle of the road I saw a motorcycle cop. He was stopped with both feet planted on the pavement, wiping some gray goo and blood off his jacket. In the middle of the plaza a guy in a suit was poking at a piece of disturbed turf. His identically suited friend kicked at the sod and picked something up. He put it in his pocket and they walked away.

No one seemed to be in charge and cops were scattering all over. One was running up the grassy slope toward the white picket fence and a bunch were ringing the book depository. Others seemed confused and paralyzed by what they'd witnessed.

A guy came running along the sidewalk and cannoned into my stroller, tripping and going flying into the street.

"You crazy woman," he screamed at me.

"Hey!" I shouted back as he sat up and grabbed his ankle. "You almost hit my baby."

I bent down making cooing noises and fussed with the blanket.

Seven - the present

Sara looked sideways from her laptop at her hunched shadow on the wall. She straightened her back, groaned, and lifted her hands from the keyboard. She wiggled her fingers like rabbit ears in the light of the desk lamp. Editing was always the pits; much harder than the initial writing.

When she'd started the first draft she had been excited with how well the characters and plot had flowed. Sometimes she'd get stuck waiting for inspiration, but she always kept her butt glued to the chair. That was how she'd managed to grind out her first four novels. Now that she'd taken the plunge and dropped her day job she had more time for writing but editing was still a grind. The fun had gone out of the book. She was tired of checking tenses, points of view, plot details and grammar. She couldn't wait for her favorite task, the last one, of giving the work over to the spellchecker. Once that was finished she could type 'The End'.

But for now she took a slug of cold coffee. It didn't help. She got up, went in the bathroom, and splashed cold water on her face. That did help. As she stared at her reflection in the mirror she realized she was also bored with her shoulder length brown hair. She wondered if she looked older than her 32 years and then noticed a frown line she hadn't seen before. Set above her brown eyes her forehead was pale from being inside while she was pounding on the keyboard instead of being out in the sun.

She was trying to find a way to describe one of the characters in her book and thought about using the mirror reflection method but decided it was too clichéd. She'd have to find some other way. She sat back down on the chair and looked round the bedroom. In contrast to the rest of the apartment it was bland and featureless, no pictures, no character; the kind of room that TV interior designers love to use in 'before' shots to demonstrate their prowess compared with the 'after' pictures. When her friend Anji had offered the use of her spare room, Sara had accepted immediately. She'd worked on the first draft in the mountain cabin but then she had needed a change of scene. City life wasn't Sara's first choice, but the apartment was roomy and warm. She'd been there three weeks now, and because Anji let her stay free of charge, 'You can pay me back when the book's a best-seller', she'd just given her the first few chapters to read.

Two hours later Sara was in full flow hammering at the keyboard when she heard Anji's footsteps on the hardwood floor of the hallway. For once her electronic 'red ink' had been flying across the pages and the buttered toast she'd made earlier was cold on the plate beside her.

Anji came in clutching the sheaf of manuscript pages and Sara saw that the few crinkles in her face had deepened. Anji flopped onto the bed.

"God what's that smell? Did you burn your toast?" Anji asked.

Sara poked at the brittle mess with one finger. "I guess it is a bit dark; must have left it too long. So what do you think of the first chapters?"

"Not bad, darling."

"What do you mean 'not bad'?" Sara said.

"Well..."

"Come on, Anji. Spit it out."

Anji pursed her lips. "Well...I'm sorry, but it's just too unbelievable."

Anji was something in the City, good with numbers and data, great with black and white issues, but she had trouble with shades of gray. She had a problem keeping men around long enough to see her good points, so she rarely had long term relationships. Guys loved her looks and she quickly went through a succession of dates. That didn't mean she didn't enjoy sex, far from it; they had adjoining bedrooms and Sara had become used to Anji's selection of endearments. But few of the men came back more than twice.

Sara waited as Anji waved the pages at her.

"What's unbelievable?" Sara said.

"Where do I start? A female sniper in the early sixties? It doesn't compute. Women weren't even burning their bras back then and most were stay at home Moms. The pretty ones were allowed to work in lobbies and reception areas and the rest were hidden away in typing pools. The few like us who had been to college were allowed to be librarians, teachers and nurses. But this woman as an assassin? And an expert with a rifle? Forget it."

Sara breathed out and smiled. "Thanks, Anji. That's great. If you don't think it's likely then no one back then would have thought so either. Ergo, it's a good plot."

"Ergo?' Anji said. "Ergo? Who talks like that except for a novelist with too many words?"

"Mea culpa," Sara said, laughing.

Anji screwed up her face and glared at Sara.

Sara looked right back, laughed, and said, "Anything else?"

"Yeah, how come she shot Kennedy?"

"There's more to come, but I'm still building the mystery. When you read the whole book you'll understand the nuances."

"If you say so. Now, all this stuff on the knoll. Would it have been possible? Two shooters hiding behind the fence and not being seen? The sewer grating? The fake Secret Service agent? The station wagon?"

"I've read a lot of assassination books, Anji. People have suggested all kinds of ideas."

"Conspiracy theorists? Like those nuts who think the CIA planned 9/11?"

"Well, yeah, But you got to admit it makes for an interesting novel. What else?"

"Okay. What's all this Tampa and Chicago stuff? I never heard of that before."

Sara frowned. "That's all been documented but not much was known about it in 1963. It was too embarrassing for the authorities. The FBI and Secret Service made so many screw-ups that only emerged years later. But I have to admit that some of the detail is writer's license."

"Okay. So when can I read the rest?"

"I've edited a few more chapters. Here you go."

"Cool. But I'm exhausted now. Are you done for this evening?"

The Woman on the Knoll

"I guess."
"Good. Let's open some wine."

Eight

The guy rolling in the gutter seemed to realize for the first time that he'd fallen over a stroller. He had the grace to look guilty, stood up, and hobbled to the sidewalk.

"Sorry, Ma'am," he said and came closer to look in the stroller.

I tried to play it cool and got in his way, fussing over the baby and making soothing noises. I faced him and changed the subject.

"What happened back there?"

"You didn't hear? They shot the president. I never liked the son of a bitch but still, he didn't deserve that."

That seemed to need a reply so I said, "Wow. Who did it? Did they catch him?"

"You think I was going to hang around to find out? There were shots going off in all directions and people running everywhere."

Then I noticed a couple of cops taking an interest in us.

The guy was talking non-stop. "Those limos are going to need new rubber after the smoke they made peeling out. And I don't understand why the motorcade slowed down when the shots were fired."

The Woman on the Knoll

"Did it?" I said. "Look, I need to get home and feed the baby. Can you let me past?"

"Sure. Sorry about knocking into you."

I pushed the stroller away from him and along the sidewalk. Behind me I heard the cops stop the guy.

"Hey, buddy, did you see what happened?"

"Yeah. They blew the president away."

"What do you mean, 'They'?"

"I was standing on the sidewalk in front of that thing up there..."

"The pergola?"

"Yeah. I heard shots coming from the building on the left and then more from behind me."

"You sure about that?"

"Yeah."

"Okay, you come with me. Fred, go talk to that woman with the stroller."

I turned as the cop caught up with me.

"Excuse me, Ma'am."

Nine

  I smelled the cop before he reached me. I didn't want to be remembered and forced myself not to react to his body odor. Hadn't he seen the ads for those new aerosol deodorants?
  "Yes?" I said.
  "I just need to ask you a few questions," he said.
  "Yes?" I said again.
  "Did you see what happened back there? In the Plaza?"
  "No, officer, I didn't... My baby was crying but I looked up when I heard the shots and saw the chaos. All that shouting and screaming was terrible. Do you know if the president is okay?"
  "No Ma'am, I don't. Did you hear where the shots came from, or how many there were?"
  Good questions.
  "I think I heard four, Officer, but I have no idea where they came from. Echoes were bouncing all over."
  "Did you see or hear anything else?"
  "No, I'm sorry."
  "Okay. Can you tell me where you were standing when the motorcade came through the plaza?"

The Woman on the Knoll

Great question. Where could I have been standing?

"I was on the sidewalk close to that brick building near the corner of Elm."

"And you couldn't tell where the shots came from?"

I could hear doubt in his voice. So much for trying to not be memorable.

"Like I said, I heard shots but the sounds were confusing. One of them might have come from up in the building behind me."

"That would be the Texas State Book Depository?"

"If that's the red brick building, yes."

"And that's all you noticed?"

"Yes officer."

He looked at me as if to say something more, but then we heard a bunch more sirens arriving in the plaza. "Okay, Ma'am. Then I'll be on my way. Thank you."

I breathed a sigh of relief.

I had a hard time getting to the apartment. The stroller was perfect camouflage as I negotiated barriers, cops, and more suits with bulging coats, but each check took longer in the rush of people fleeing the scene. My adrenalin rush had crashed and I think shock set in for while. I squeezed hard on the stroller handles to stop my hands and arms from trembling, and staggered a little on the sidewalk.

"Hey, you okay?" A big handyman type was leaning over a yard wall watching me. "You need a shot?" He held up a bottle. "I know I do."

I was tempted but I had to keep moving for David's sake.

"Thanks, but no."

He slurred after me,

"We finally got the bastard. I don't wish it on Jackie, she don't deserve it, but he damn near started World War Three over those Cuban nukes."

"Get lost, jerk," I muttered as I hurried round a corner. I turned into the driveway of the apartment complex with minutes to spare before the 2 pm deadline. I shoved the stroller under the stairs and ran to the apartment. When I saw that the door was open I paused.

It didn't make sense.

I waited a while longer but didn't hear anything so I stepped in. My brain flared when I saw the dark red splashes coating the table.

"Oh no."

My legs buckled and I sank to the floor, staring vacantly at the blood that had dripped off the table and pooled on the floor. I couldn't take my eyes off it. I couldn't not smell it. I leaned forward, touched it and raised my finger to my mouth. I was sure it was David's. Maybe all I'd ever find of him.

The bastards.

They'd promised.

I felt my tongue rubbing my upper lip, tasting his blood, feeling the texture of him.

Then I realized I wasn't alone in the room.

"Hey," said a voice behind me.

Ten

David and I were together for just six months, until the end of October. I guess he saw something that he liked in me. I certainly did in him. He was my best; considerate, but wild when I needed it, soft and gentle when I whimpered in his ear. He was tall, dark, and handsome...no not really, but he was tall, good looking, and blond.

We first met in San Francisco but traveled all over: to the Caribbean, Europe and the Mediterranean, and then back cross country. Death Valley and the south-west deserts allured us for weeks, the dry and hot a beautiful change from the green humidity and the smells and spices of foreign cities. Space, quiet, and views that went on forever trapped us in a desert spell.

We had a great life until we came back to New Orleans. David had spent time there and had lots of drinking friends. He often went out with them would usually come back feeling no pain.

But one evening he went out and didn't return. He'd done that once before but he came back the next day with a huge hangover. He brought me some flowers and then took a whole day to sleep it off. He was an idiot, but I loved him. We'd been planning another trip, this time to

Hawaii, but we never made it.

I spent the morning wondering where he was. I called the numbers of the friends that I knew, but none of them had been out drinking with David the night before. I went and visited the bars in the neighborhood without success. No-one had seen him, or they just weren't telling me. When I got home I found a note that had been pushed under the door. It was written on cheap paper with one of those new ballpoint pen things. The ink had smeared and the envelope was crumpled but the message was simple.

'Do you want David back?'

There was no address, no phone number, and no name. Nothing to indicate who had sent it or what they wanted.

I waited all evening slumped on the couch. The bastard waited six hours before calling late that night.

"Hello?"

"This is David's friend." His voice sounded gravelly, low pitched, and menacing.

"Who?"

"Tony, the friend he's staying with. I'll put him on."

David's voice, so familiar, but quavering and stressed, said, "Tell them you'll do it, Jan, whatever they want."

I could scarcely hear him. "What? David! What's happening? Where are you?"

David's 'friend' Tony came back on the phone. "We need you to do a job. And we'll cut more bits off of him if you contact the cops."

"What do you mean...?"

"We'll call later. Look outside your door."

The Woman on the Knoll

The phone went dead. I collapsed back on the couch. I couldn't think what to do. I was three thousand miles from my old friends back in San Francisco and calling them made no sense. They were always broke and couldn't afford to fly out, and anyway, they were always stoned.

I opened the apartment door. The innocuous brown paper package lying outside had no stamps or a return address. Inside I found a gift wrapped box containing a nest of cotton. When I pulled it out a bloody finger fell on the floor, dried crust sticking some of the cotton to the stump. I screamed and fainted.

Eleven

I looked up from David's blood on the floor. I was still on my knees, memories of the severed finger racing through my brain. That had been one month ago, and started the chain of events that led me to Dallas on November 22nd., 1963.

"Hey," he said again.

The rough southern accent sounded familiar and I remembered hearing it in the background of one of the phone calls. Before I could move a huge weight crushed me to the floor as he pushed me forward and sat on my back. He pinned my shoulders with his knees. I couldn't move or breathe. I jerked when he ran his fingers through my hair. Though I could hardly move he obviously felt my reaction and slapped me across the back of my head. Then I felt cold metal on my neck, pressing in hard.

"Tony sent me," he said. "He thought you might be clever enough to get away. He really wanted you to be the second Lee."

Second Lee? What the hell did that mean?

"What...?" I tried to speak with the little breath left in my lungs.

I felt the pressure of the gun barrel increase as he

leaned forward and smacked me on the head again.

He laughed. "What...?" he said, in a parody of my choking sound.

"Where's David?" I managed to say.

That got me another cuff on the head.

"The last time I saw him he was okay." He giggled as though he'd made a huge joke and I felt him shaking on top of me as he laughed louder. Then he said, "Where's the rifle?"

His weight on my back seemed heavier as I tried to breathe, let alone speak. He hit me again.

"Where's the rifle, bitch?"

I gurgled as best I could.

"What?"

I guess he got the message then because the pressure on my back eased as he slid his knees to each side of my body. "You've got ten seconds, Jan."

I hadn't thought he could skewer me harder with the gun but the pain became excruciating.

"Okay, I'll tell you." I was trying to think of a logical place where I could have hidden it, but where it wouldn't be accessible.

"Well?"

"You probably haven't talked to Johnny yet," I said. "I imagine he's on the plane out of here by now."

"What's it got to do with Johnny?"

"He must have heard it."

"Heard what?"

"The noise of the rifle when I dropped it into the sewer. I wish I'd been quicker and shot him with it."

I wondered if he'd buy it and decided to complicate the issue. "But the cops will be swarming all over the area now. They're bound to find it."

"I don't believe you. That gun wouldn't have fitted between the bars."

I called his bluff. "How would you know? It was only Johnny and me who went up there to check out the escape route."

His weight increased as he sank down on my back again. The guy was heavy but it wasn't his brain that weighed a lot. I could almost hear his gray matter sloshing as I tried to baffle him with bullshit. I was finding it ever harder to speak, but I managed. "Or maybe I stashed it somewhere else."

By now I'd figured out that for some reason I was safe as long as they thought I could get them the rifle.

He squirmed on top of me and was quiet for the longest time. If I could have held my breath in suspense I would have. Soon he wouldn't need to shoot me to keep me quiet.

"You're full of it, Jan."

I felt the pressure of the barrel even more. I didn't have much time. Then the pressure eased. I guess the lunk was trying to think.

"Okay," he said, "but Tony isn't worried about any damage in transit. Up on your knees."

"What?"

"Shut up!"

He pulled me up on my knees and fumbled for my jeans belt and buttons. I took my weight on my right hand and slid my left down my leg.

Then he fell back screaming.

The one thing I'll ever thank my father for is his advice about having a back up plan. The pop of the twenty-two I'd pulled from my ankle holster seemed quiet for the amount of damage it caused to his kneecap. Splinters of bone stuck out from the side and he was rolling in agony. He grabbed his knee with both hands.

I spun round and grabbed the pistol he'd dropped. Then I eased away from him, sat up, and watched him carefully.

"Where's David?" I said.

He shook his head. I answered him with a smack on his broken knee. He screamed and I thrust the barrel of the twenty-two into his mouth. He gagged and writhed but eventually quieted down.

"Where's David? What have you done with him?"

He looked at me with glazed eyes and tried to smile around the gun barrel.

I saw the blood from his knee was about to mingle with David's and I clubbed him with the butt of his own gun until he moved away and the danger of his miserable body fluids mixing with David's was reduced. At the time I felt it was important.

"Is David OK?"

I was up on my feet, the adrenalin kicking in again and I held the revolver directed at his groin. I kept far enough away so he couldn't reach me. He groaned and then screamed with pain. My kicking his injured leg might have had something to do with that. Around this time I started to wonder if any of this noise might have alarmed the neighbors but in this low rent part of the city it wasn't unusual to hear arguments and screams. I figured I'd be okay because all l could hear was radios and televisions on full blast as the news of JFK's shooting spread.

"What's your name?"

"What do you care, bitch."

"The bitch has a gun, buster."

I gave him another kick and heard an even louder scream.

"Alright, alright. I'm Joe."

This was an improvement.

"Okay Joe, tell me about David."

His eyes blinked and I could almost see his brain checking the odds of getting away with believable lies versus the further pain he might get. His brow cleared and I looked for any eye aversion that would give him away.

"He's not here."

"Don't be stupid, Joe."

"Look, I didn't do nuthin, right? Tony did it."

I pointed at the floor.

"Is this David's blood?"

His look of pain shifted to a crafty flickered opening of his eyes. Wider than when he was dealing with the pain.

"No."

This was so ridiculous I fired again and hit the toes of his other leg. His howling went on longer this time and now he had both legs tight to his chest. He screamed, "Yes, it's David's."

I waited until he was only sobbing and then shouted through his misery.

"Be reasonable, Joe. You don't need all this pain."

He turned even paler and his eyes flickered to my pistol. I didn't want to go too far but I needed the whole truth. I had a question and wasn't sure how I'd handle the answer.

"What's happened to David?"

"I don't know…"

Another tap on his leg.

He sucked in a huge breath. His knee was leaking more blood now and it was running through his fingers.

I wiggled the pistol at him and pointed it higher on his body, back to the groin.

"Who are you more scared of, Joe. Me or Tony? Here's a clue. I'm here, Tony isn't. Work it out."

He gulped. "They left a few hours ago."

His voice tailed off in pain but he saw the anger in my eyes.

"No," he said, as I raised the twenty-two toward his head and took up the pressure on the trigger. He tried to edge backwards but squealed and howled. I was getting annoyed by his noise now, and figured that even round here the neighbors would be getting suspicious.

I could smell the fear coming from him, even overpowering the sickly taint of blood in the room. I got down on my knees and put my face in his. He didn't even have the strength to make a move for the pistol. Onion and garlic hit me.

"Don't shoot," he croaked, "I'll tell you."

I waited.

"David…"

"Yes?"

"He…he tried to escape and Tony shot him."

"And?" I didn't want to hear the truth but I needed to. He groaned.

"He's dead."

I stared at him. I couldn't do anything else. Everything that I'd done had been predicated on a lie. I would kill Tony for this. I looked at Joe's contorted, scared face and almost pulled the trigger. He realized it and managed to move back a couple of inches before he slumped again. The twin pools of blood, one bright red, the other brown and sticky, finally mingled.

"Don't do a thing," I said.

Despite the pain he knew that his life hung by a thread. I saw his attention flicker between the gun and my face. Then his eyes closed and his breathing shallowed. I hit his knee with the edge of my hand and this time he hardly yelped.

I staggered back, fell into a chair across the room from him and collapsed. I pictured David's smiling face above me as we made love, and I wallowed in misery. He'd been so full of life as we'd traveled the world. We'd traveled first class and he always found the best local restaurants. Why did I think of that now? He'd put his arm around me in the gondola as we cruised at night through the oil lamp illuminated canals past architecture that mocked our pathetic American attempts at grandeur. He'd kissed me in what I'd thought of as classical Venetian behavior and in our hotel that night with its high ceilings and four poster bed we'd damn near flattened the mattress. I sighed. At Furnace Creek we thought we couldn't ever be hotter, until we went to Badwater, two hundred feet below sea-level. Why did I think of that too? We'd never do anything together again. I glanced at Joe. He hadn't moved and the blood had almost stopped leaking out of him. I couldn't care less.

I sat for ten minutes, maybe twenty, until I worked out that Joe was probably due to call Tony after he'd found me and the rifle. I pondered this for a while. Now I knew the truth I wasn't sure I wanted to leave. I kicked Joe's leg

The Woman on the Knoll

hard and was surprised when he groaned. I crept close to him.

"Where is his body?"

He jerked and I knew he could hear me.

"Come on Joe. Where is he? I'm going to shoot you again if I don't get the truth from you. "I hit his bad knee with the pistol butt. Got a pretty good scream out of him this time. "How much pain do you want Joe? "

His lips were dry. He licked and muttered, "I don't know where."

"When did he die? "

Nothing.

"When did Tony kill David?" I was shouting now and the neighbors must have been least curious.

"Yesterday."

Jesus! He'd been dead before I fired in Dealey Plaza. I wasn't even being coerced at the time I'd been shooting.

"Why would Tony do that?"

Joe groaned and slumped even lower to the floor.

"Why?"

"Because of the manhunt after the assassination. He said it would be huge."

Manhunt. Jesus. All I'd thought about for the last hour was David. I'd never thought past getting him back and now it might cost me my life. For a moment I considered just giving in to the despair, but then they would have won and I wouldn't be writing this record of the whole miserable affair. So I focused on revenge and that carried me through the next few days.

I'd had no backup plan for this eventuality but I did see one bright spot. Joe gave it to me - they would be searching for a man. That's why it's called a manhunt.

Joe gave a huge groan and lay still. Then I heard him fart. Assuming he'd died I gave him another kick just for good measure. Then, dammit, he groaned again. Not dead, huh. Shame.

I checked in the mirror before I left and wiped a smear of blood off my cheek. The small patch I noticed on my shirt was masked by the plaid pattern. Outside the apartment I retrieved the baby stroller and checked that the rifle parts were still concealed. I didn't know if I'd need either again or why I'd keep any kind of evidence with me, but I did. Who said I had to be rational? I'd been part of an assassination conspiracy, Joe had tried to kill me but I'd tortured him instead, and then I'd discovered my lover was dead. I had a little cash plus the twenty-seven dollars I'd found on Joe. I had no friends in this town and I needed out.

I pushed the stroller furiously along the sidewalk, with no idea where I was going and not caring. My manic phase faded and my speed and my brain slowed enough to catch up with each other. Perhaps it would be better to hole up somewhere? But if I did then Tony would eventually find me. He didn't own this town but he knew the people who did. At the moment he probably thought I was out of the way; either caught in Dealey Plaza or dead at the apartment. Maybe his guys wouldn't yet be watching the bus station, but what about the feds? Screw it. I decided to try. I mean, who would shoot a president and leave town on a bus?

The Woman on the Knoll

Twelve

The bus station was packed and I was exhausted when I reached it. The white crowd had plenty of comfortable seating and our restroom was conveniently placed just down the corridor. The colored clerk at the counter was sniffling as she helped me while on the other side of the hall her brothers and sisters in segregation had to sit on their suitcases and bags. Their restrooms were outside.

A radio was announcing the latest news about the 36th President. Lyndon Baines Johnson was on Air Force One heading back to Washington with the ex-First Lady, Jackie Kennedy. The 35th President's coffin was also on board. People were talking non stop, like everyone was stuck on transmit.

"JFK was going to fix this country for us," a guy in a black suit said.

"Did you see Jackie's face?"

"Where was the Secret Service? Aren't they supposed to stop this kind of thing?"

"I wouldn't want to be the guy in charge of security now."

"What about the FBI?"

Good question, I thought.

"That poor woman. Did you see her pink suit?"

"She was so brave."

"On TV I saw her trying to escape over the back of the car."

"No. She was trying to grab a piece of JFK's brain."

I burst into tears and couldn't bear to listen anymore. What had we done today? But where had the FBI or the Secret Service been? Why hadn't they done anything to stop it?

I tried to keep myself from thinking about David but he was constantly in my brain. At the ticket counter I heard the radio newscaster mention the cold war and the communist threat in light of Kennedy's death.

The guy in line behind me, a Hispanic, was spouting off. "I'm not surprised. Those anti-Castro groups went nuts when Kennedy didn't send any support for the Bay of Pigs invasion of Cuba. I reckon one of them got him."

From the colored line on the far side one old lady was keening and wailing over and over that Martin Luther King Jr. would be next and how all the good people died young.

Crap, I thought. Lots of people die young.

Then we heard over the radio, "The lone gunman who shot and killed President Kennedy from the sixth floor of the Texas School Book Depository building has been caught."

Lone gunman? What the hell?

"Lee Harvey Oswald was arrested in a Dallas movie theater where he'd fled after also killing Officer Tippit of the Dallas Police Department."

The Woman on the Knoll

They say that everyone knows where they were when JFK was shot, and obviously I do. But the moment when Lee's name was announced in the bus station is engraved in my brain. If they could find him that quickly then how much longer before they caught me. Lee knew all of us; me, Johnny, Marv, and Tony. Thank God I'd kept the stroller idea to myself. I stayed in line and bought my ticket.

When we boarded the bus I had to pick up the baby and also fold the stroller without the rifle being spotted. The driver helped me but he was too busy stressing to notice anything peculiar about the umbrella holder. I hurried inside the bus, grabbing a seat in the Whites Only section.

'They'll spit on our Civil Rights now," said a black guy as he moved up the bus. "At least Oswald was white. Just imagine if…" His voice tailed away.

"Holy shit...I hadn't thought of that," his girlfriend said. "Jeez..."

A middle-aged lady wiping tears from her eyes, followed. She stopped and waved toward the seat by me. I didn't want company, but the bus was filling up and refusing her would make me stand out. She slumped alongside me and whimpered into her handkerchief. I shifted my baby bundle away from her and stared into the night, my mind a blur of fear, dread, and guilt.

The journey took two hours and my anxiety grew with each mile. Eventually the woman next to me recovered her composure and wanted to help me by holding the baby.

I went from "Thanks, but I don't want to wake her up," to "She's not happy with strangers."

I stared out the window at the dark, ignoring the occasional whispered words of shock from nearby seats. The upheaval and the chaos of the Bus Station was left behind and replaced by the emptiness of sudden loss. Everyone on the bus was grieving. I wept silently.

I jumped and jerked away when the woman beside me clutched my arm.

"Are you alright dear?"

I ignored her, sighed, and closed my eyes, wishing the old bat would leave me alone.

She had just said, "I wish you'd let me help..." when the driver turned on the radio.

The low chatter in the bus stopped.

I heard more of those phrases which are now ingrained in that generation's memory. Against a background of traffic noise, sirens, shouts and tears, the newscasters' recordings kept repeating,

'The president's been shot,'

'Jackie was at his side'

'lone gunman'

'her pink suit'

'people ran toward the grassy knoll'

That was a new one; the first time that I realized I'd been standing on a knoll.

'left at high speed heading for Parkland hospital'

'no response from the Kennedy compound'

'Officer Tippit was slain'

'received the news of the president's death at 1:45 this afternoon'

'Lee Harvey Oswald arrested'

'LBJ was sworn in on Air Force One'

'in the movie theater without a shot being fired'

The Woman on the Knoll

'pulled back from the trunk of the limo'

I phased everything out and wept some more. The journey ended. I waited till the passengers in front of me had all got off before I unfolded my cramped body from the seat. I motioned for the next person to pass in front of me before I moved to the aisle but the bus driver shouted, 'Come on lady, you're the last.'

I looked back and realized everyone else was colored. I opened my mouth to object but remembered I shouldn't draw attention to myself, and moved into the aisle with a murmured 'sorry' to the bearded man I'd displaced in line.

As I headed for the exit I heard him whisper at my back, "One day lady, one day..."

I got off the bus and gulped when I saw the driver pushing the stroller toward me.

"Thanks."

"No problem Ma'am, you just get her home. What a world to bring a child up in."

He moved away, leaving the coloreds to grab their own cases from the hold.

I walked downtown, bought a bottle of whisky in a corner store, and checked into one of those new motels with the six dollar rate. Once I was in my room I grabbed the bottle that I'd stuffed in the seat alongside the baby bundle and shoved the stroller into the corner of the room. I poured a stiff drink into a glass from the bathroom and then into me. I gave up thinking and concentrated on the bottle. I must have fallen asleep because next morning I woke up cold with a headache fit to burst. I grabbed another drink, got into the bed, pulled up the covers, and noticed the stroller was on its side. When did that happen?

The pounding on the door hours, or minutes later, woke me. I almost made it to the bathroom before I threw up.

The banging continued.

"What?" I shouted, or tried to. All I could manage was a gargled noise.

"Maid Service."

"Later."

"But Ma'am, it's eleven o'clock and you were due out at ten."

Shit. "Book me in for another night and I'll come pay this afternoon."

"Sorry Ma'am, but the manager will want paying now."

"Give me an hour?"

"OK ma'am, but no more or the manager will give me a rash of… Sorry. He'll be on at noon, so if you can do it before then?"

"Alright, I'm coming." I staggered to the door and stuffed seven dollars into her hand. I saw her name tag and said, "I'll pick up the receipt later, Gabriella."

I wasn't hungry and I didn't feel like taking a shower but I thought coffee would help. "Gabriella? There's fifty cents for you if you can get me some coffee."

She brought me some burnt liquid five minutes later.

I lay on the bed and let the events of yesterday wash all over me. Had Joe been yanking my chain? Was David really dead? I turned on the radio for some mind deadening noise but all I could find was a rehash of yesterday's news. The hacks were all spouting the phrases I'd heard on the bus and the country seemed to have

The Woman on the Knoll

stopped.

I rushed into the small bathroom and got to the toilet just in time to throw up again. The coffee tasted worse this time. I went back to bed and pulled the blankets up.

David's face, Daddy's and Uncle Jed's flickered through my dreams. I don't know why David's was associated with the other two. I hated that they had pushed me down this path. David was the only bright spot in my nightmare. When I woke up sweaty, with the bedding trashed all round me I drank some water and took a shower. I spent the rest of the day in a daze.

Next morning was a repeat of the day before. Gabriella gave me an extra hour. I showered again, not believing how sweaty I was, towelled dry and left. I walked ten blocks and used a payphone to call Tony's number.

"You double-crossing bastard!"

"Hey, nice to hear from you, Jan. We were worried you'd got lost. David's here. Why don't you come and get him." My wild roller coaster of emotion was messing with my stomach and hangover again.

His words hit me and I staggered. "But Joe said he was already dead." This was all too crazy.

"You've got it wrong, Jan. David's fine; it's Joe that's dead."

Joe was dead? But he'd been okay when I left him. "Who killed him? Shit I don't care. Let me speak to David."

"Not that easy, Jan. You have to come here to do that."

"Bastard," I said. "Why can't you just let him go?"

"Sorry Jan. He's having trouble walking without two toes."

I heard my own intake of breath and almost dropped the phone.

He went on. "You did well, Jan. Where are you now?"

"Like I'd tell you. Why did you set me up?"

"What gave you that idea? Johnny messed up, he wasn't supposed to abandon you. Come back and we'll sort all this out."

"You're full of it, Tony. Joe botched his job and you just want to finish it off."

"Why would we do that, Jan? Everything went so well."

"Shut up! You know that Lee couldn't shoot well enough to hit Kennedy from the sixth floor, that's why you had Johnny and Marv in those other locations. You set me up just like you did Lee. He was supposed to get caught in the TSBD but somehow he got away. I've no idea how you maneuvered him into getting caught, and what was it with that Tibbet thing? You did well Tony, but there's no way you're getting me as well. Lee was a fall guy to divert attention from Johnny and Marv, just like me on the knoll. Johnny made sure I was stuck up there to be the second patsy."

"Don't you think that knoll is a cute word, Jan? It never would have occurred to me, but when UPI used it the press glommed onto it."

"Goddammit! You set us both up. When I escaped you sent Joe to the apartment to kill me, didn't you?"

"So when do you want to come fetch your precious David, huh?"

"Prove he's still alive."

"Jan, I already told you…"

"Prove it."

"Wait a minute…"

The phone crackled and then I heard David's voice. "Jan, are you okay?"

His voice sounded weak and thready. I burst into tears.

Tony came back on the phone. "Okay Jan. You coming to get him?"

I heard him through my sobbing and tried to figure out what to do. But I had no ideas. I couldn't think of a single way for David and me to get out of this. I laid down the phone and heard Tony shouting. I staggered and swayed to the side of the phone booth. I would have sunk to my knees without its support. If I went to meet them they'd kill us both, even assuming David was still alive by then. I had no way of telling what kind of trap I might walk into. But without David I was hopeless. There was no other option.

"You still there?"

I tried to sound upbeat but I heard the desperation in my voice. "When and where?"

"Where are you now?"

I almost told him before I stopped myself. "Uh-huh…."

"Okay. Let's meet downtown in Dover in three hours."

"No," I said, more firmly than I would have thought possible. There was no way I could get there by then. "Make it 6 pm and be on your own with David."

"Deal. Make it by the Museum gates."

Thirteen

I went to a local bank and rented a safety deposit box. I had to open an account, fill out a couple of forms, and give them a deposit. I had a year before another payment was due. The assistant who'd helped me with the forms opened the gate, led me to a windowless cubicle, and then brought me a lockable box. I'd made sure they had a box big enough before I signed the forms.

"Anything else I can do before I leave you to it?"

"No thanks, this looks perfect."

He left, closing the door behind him.

I pulled the rifle from the stroller holster. The parts fitted in the box and I added the box of cartridges before closing the lid. When I knocked on the door, Harold, the cashier, led me through a huge vault door and to a wall of safety boxes.

"Some of these are six feet long," Harold said. "The safe had to be made special for us. There are a lot of hunters in town and some of their wives won't stand for guns in the house."

"I can believe it,' I said.

"Of course, they all need the longer boxes. Yours wouldn't take more than an umbrella." He laughed at his

The Woman on the Knoll

own joke and I tried to humor him with a smile.

He slid the box into slot #395, closed the door, twisted the two keys in opposite directions and gave me one. Then he ushered me through the gate with old fashioned courtesy and made as though to check out the baby.

"She's got a terrible cold," I said, pulling the blanket further up her face.

He jumped back, "Oh, well I shouldn't take that back to my kids should I? Well goodbye Mrs..." His voice tailed off as he'd obviously forgotten my name.'

I filled in the blank for him, "Kennedy," I said.

"Oh yes, of course." He pulled a face. "Such a sad week."

He looked close to tears as I walked away. Around the corner I walked into an alley and at last I was able to dump the stroller and the baby bundle. I regretted not having the disguise, but soon someone was going to wonder why Mom was pushing a china doll around.

I walked into another maelstrom of chaos in the bus station. People clustered in small groups, some with their transistors against their ears, others talking animatedly.

"What's happening?" I said to a young man in a crumpled suit ahead of me.

"I just heard on the radio. That Lee Harvey Oswald, the guy who assassinated President Kennedy, he's been shot."

"What?"

His face creased with emotion. "Some guy has killed him."

I didn't understand. Lee had been in police

custody. How could he be dead?

"Deputies were transferring him from Police Headquarters to the Dallas County Jail. They were in the basement on the way to the police van when some guy pulled a gun and shot him. The stupid thing is, the killer never tried to escape, he just stood there waiting to be arrested."

Damn! Lee had survived for only two days before they shut his mouth. They'd do the same to me and David if I made the meeting. We were walking corpses.

I didn't go to Dover that day and I've never been back to Texas. I abandoned David and got the next bus out of town. Cold logic told me there was no point in us both dying but I still have nightmares over that decision. I loved David with all my heart, but I guess I loved me more. I cried all the way out of the state.

Fourteen

The phone call went even worse than I expected.
"Daddy, it's Jan..."
"Who?"
"Jan, your daughter."
"What daughter?"
"Daddy..."
"The one who ran off five years ago? Never sent a letter or a postcard? Never called at Thanksgiving or Christmas. Didn't show up for her mother's funeral? Where the hell have you been all this time and why are you...?"

I put down the phone.

I sat on a bench looking out over the toxic dump of the sullen, brown, Mogul River. Mom was dead too? That made three in three days. Kennedy, Lee, and now mom. Probably David and me next. I tried to stand but my legs felt like Jell-O. I slumped back on the bench. How many more deaths? I hadn't even asked when mom had died. She'd been a quiet, unassuming woman, cowed by daddy but often able to get her way when she thought he pushed us too hard. But she always failed to stop him taking us to the shooting range.

"You can give the girls self-defense classes but no

guns. They'll use them over my dead body!"

He'd listened but in his mind we weren't complete if we couldn't stand up for ourselves and so he ignored her. There were two other people I could call for help, but that would have to wait. I was in no shape for further difficult conversations. I needed time to think so I checked into the seediest motel I could find. For seediest read cheapest. I had some money but I couldn't rent a car without using my driver's license and I didn't want to leave a paper trail. By now the cops or the FBI could be after me. I fell asleep wondering how to travel without being identified. I'd been lucky on the buses so far, but public transportation would be increasingly risky.

I was woken at 3 am by a car screeching in the motel parking lot. My heart jumped. I grabbed my pistol and looked out but it was just some dork throwing his old Pontiac around like it was a Rambler Rebel. His girl didn't seem impressed but she squealed as he chased her into their room and kicked the door closed behind him.

The prospect of sex can do weird things to a guy. In this case he had forgotten to turn off his car lights, so I went out to check if he'd left the keys in the ignition. My first break in days.

The Woman on the Knoll

Fifteen

Fifteen minutes later I was ten miles away heading north. I ate a Hershey bar that I found in the glove compartment, brushed the crumbs off my jeans and started to worry about a dozen things. The car was hot and I needed serious money. My clothes were stinky because I was re-wearing them each day. Daddy was no help so Sis and Uncle Jed were the only family I had left to approach. Jed was out of the reckoning, had been for a long time now, so Sis it had to be.

The sugar high soon dumped me and by 7 am I needed to crash. I pulled off the mountain highway that was threatening my life as I half-dozed at the wheel, and drove along a dirt road into a National Forest campground. I parked in a day use area and slept in the backseat for seven hours, waking up hungry and needing to pee. The campground satisfied the latter and the next little town the former. I'd eaten in better diners but was never so grateful for food.

I drove all day and ate dinner in another diner. Similar menu, similar prices. Afterward I drove round town. The place was folksy, but with a darker side east of the freeway. The kind of area with disused railroads, old factories, psychic readers and tire shops. Among them was the perfect used car dealer, so crummy it didn't even have soggy balloons waving in the breeze. The place comprised oil stains, rusting bodywork, car hoods raised in expectation and a bald owner with a beer habit to maintain. His shirt belly-bulged and he had that overweight straight leg waddle, like he was eight months gone.

He leered at me as I drove up. "Nice car," he lied, patting it on the hood. "You selling?"

"Depends."

"On what?"

"How much you want for one of those old clunkers." I waved in the general direction of the junk in the lot.

"Hey lady, I don't deal in no old trash. These here are some of Detroit's finest."

I shut my mouth and waited.

"Is your old man gonna come down and pick one out for you?"

"If you want a sale today you'd better wash out your mouth."

His brain struggled with his pride before his wallet made the decision.

"How can I help?"

"Which of those cars back there don't have a pink slip?"

"What? They all do."

I looked at him and then at my watch. "You're just putting wrecks back together, right?"

"Who told you that?"

"Dan isn't it?" I said, using the name from the board leaning against the sagging fence.

"Yeah?"

"This Pontiac's got no pink slip either."

"And you want to…?"

"Exchange it for a cheaper car, no questions asked."

"Is it hot?"

"A bit," I said, "but it's a good car. Plenty of power and good tires."

"How far?"

"What?"

"Where d'you get it from?"

"New Mexico, plenty far enough. Put it this way. Keep it out of circulation for week or so and then sell it. I'll take that old heap in the corner if it runs."

"The green one?"

"Yes, the green one," I said, with all the patience I had left.

An hour later I drove the faded green Pukemobile down to the gas station. Dan had turned me down when I had asked for a full tank and just laughed at me. "Ged owda here."

"Remember you're gonna keep the car in the back forty."

"Yeah, yeah."

I waited in the car at the gas station. A kid in light blue striped dungarees came out wiping his hands on a rag.

"Fill her up, Ma'am?"

I nodded and he gassed up the Ford.

I sat back and looked at the few cattle in the fields lying in the pasture and chewing the cud. They looked happy with life. I felt short-changed and jealous.

When the kid came round to wash the windshield

he was smiling. He looked about seventeen and eager to please. Maybe this was his first job. He finished the screen and came to my window. "Check the oil, Ma'am?"

I nodded and waited.

Then he said, "Can you release the hood?"

"Oh, of course." I felt like an idiot as I groped under the dash.

"Let me, Ma'am."

His hand went straight to the lever and his arm brushed my leg. He blushed and almost ran to the front to raise the hood as a shield between us. I heard him grunt as he twisted the oil cap off and saw him grab a can of oil from the rack. Gurgles were followed by a slight rock of the car as he wrenched the filler cap back on. He slammed the hood down.

"Anything else Ma'am? Wash and rub down?"

He not quite leered a smile at me and now he looked like a man, not a kid.

"Rusty!" Another fat old guy appeared. "Get back here in the office."

Rusty fled, now more boy than man.

I laughed, and then the old guy wheezed to my door. He checked the pump level and said, "That's three dollars for the gas and fifty cents for the oil."

I gave him the money and he lowered his face to the window, "Did Rusty try anything?"

I shook my head and said, "Try anything? What do you mean?"

He pursed his fleshy lips and muttered, "Aw nothing. The boy's a bit cheeky to customers sometimes." He looked at the Ford. "You got this from Dan, huh?"

"How do you know that?"

"I towed it after the crash last year and Dan's had it sitting on the lot ever since."

"Great. How far to the next town?"

His mouth widened and then I saw his brown misshapen teeth as he roared with laughter. "Eighty miles that way," he pointed in the direction I was facing, "and sixty back behind you. But I wouldn't worry, this old clunker won't get that far.

He was right. Twenty-five miles down the road smoke came from under the hood and smeared the road behind with blue fumes. As I pulled over I heard a tortured metallic sound and bits of metal seemed to crash against the hood. The smoke drifted away and I saw a long puddle had followed me to the shoulder. I should have road tested the damn thing but I'd never bought a car before and had no idea what to look for.

The road was barely two lanes, not that it mattered with the traffic round there. I'd only seen two cars since leaving town and it was getting dark. I had no food or water, was scared and exhausted, and feeling crappy. My head slumped onto the steering wheel. I ignored the thump as I misjudged the distance and my forehead hit hard. The pain seemed to help.

When I raised my head I had no idea how long I'd bawled my eyes out. I groped on the roof for a switch and finally found one. The interior flooded with light and I stared at my reflection in the mirror. My hair was matted with dirt and my face was a disaster with red weepy eyes and streaked cheeks where tears had run down through the dust. I still stunk and my forehead was banging a drum in my head. I bawled again.

The car rocked. I wound up the windows as a dry

wind rolled past. I tried to list the positives. I was still alive. I was lost, but therefore Tony couldn't find me either. I had shelter for the night and I was young, fit, and healthy. I shifted in the seat and turned the interior light off. I didn't want to run the battery down.

I saw headlights in the rear view mirror and a car flashed by at high speed. I ignored the air buffet that rocked the car and watched the rear lights. They flashed brighter. Damn! The car turned round and headlights flared in my face. The car pulled beside me and the window rolled down. An interior light came on and I saw the uniform, the shot gun in its rack and the wire grill between the driver and the passenger seats.

"You okay, ma'am?"

His face was gentle but as he spoke a laugh came from behind. He turned to the two guys in the backseat that I hadn't noticed. He growled, "Quiet," and then in a more intense voice and menacing voice, he said, "I'm surprised at you for making a comment like that, Davy, and your Pa will be too."

Officer Stone, his badge visible as he turned back to me, asked again if I was alright.

"Yes thanks, officer. I was tired and stopped for a rest."

He wrinkled his nose and said, "You sure? It's kinda lonely out here."

"I'm fine, thanks."

"Have you been drinking Ma'am?" He leaned across, sniffed and recoiled. "Guess not." Banging and laughter erupted in the back seat as the radio squawked. "Shut it," Stone said, and picked up the hand set. After a one sided conversation he said, "Have to leave ma'am, I'll

The Woman on the Knoll

check back later." He swung the car in a squealing U-turn and scattered gravel as he accelerated away.

I leaned back and breathed out.

Another breeze swirled round the car and in through the open window. I grabbed the winder to roll it up when suddenly a face appeared in the opening.

I screamed.

Sixteen

"What the...? Get outa here."

I cranked the winder as fast as I could but the old mechanism, how the hell do those things work anyway, seized solid. I screamed again.

The guy outside shone a flashlight onto his face. He was young and at first I didn't recognize him without the blue dungarees, baseball cap, and gas station logo. He had curly golden hair, a little longer than was fashionable in the early 60's, and his features were smooth in the loom of the flashlight. I still fought the window winder.

"Need some help, Ma'am?"

I paused in my struggle as I recognized his voice.

"Rusty? You scared me to half to death!"

"More than Tom?"

"Who?"

"Tom Stone, the cop."

"Yes, dammit!"

I gave up on the winder, grabbed the door handle and pushed hard. He staggered back as the door hit him. He backed off as I flung myself out of the car and swung my fist. Daddy and Jed would have been appalled at my lack of coordination, but I caught him on the neck and he staggered. I launched myself at him and then...nothing.

I came round in a vehicle. One with an engine that didn't bang or rattle. Refreshing. I was reclined in the seat, warm, and being lullabied by a country station. The songs were all about pickup trucks, beer, lost loves, and ma dawg.

I opened my eyes and looked around. "Stop! Let me out!"

The tires squealed on the blacktop and the truck shuddered, then we were sliding on gravel. Before we stopped I was out of the door, down on all fours and throwing up. I hate puking, especially after too much booze, but this was worse. This was condensed fear and fast food, washed up with stress and fatigue.

I felt a hand on my shoulder and instinctively jerked away.

"You okay, Ma'am?"

I rolled on my side, away from the mess, and curled up, my arms round my legs. I don't think Rusty knew what to do, but he did it well. He went back to the truck and returned with a blanket that he threw over me. He waited while I upchucked again. The second time was worse and I felt a familiar cold sweat. Rusty's hands went around and under me. I barely had the strength to protest before he had me back in the cab. He turned the heater up high while I snuggled in the blanket.

I was drowsing when he pulled me out of the truck. He supported me with an arm round my waist and I let him lead me up a few stairs, shuffle me through a door, and lower me to a bed. I was oblivious to my surroundings and shivered as my clothes were taken off me.

I woke up naked and warm under a huge pile of

blankets. A hotter shape was lying by my side, compressing the covers. My body ached and my brain had given up on me. I shut down again. Uncle Jed and David blurred through dreams, of Jackie's pink and JFK's slump, my rifle and its ammo, and my sister's face. She walked in on the dream then beckoned and turned away. I heard metal clattering.

Next time I woke in a huge sweat and rolled over, right into a warm body. The metal clattering continued as I opened my eyes, looking straight at a furry chest topped by the hugest brown eyes I'd ever seen. The dog's tongue came out and licked my forehead.

"His name is Colt and he's friendly, but don't encourage him."

I saw Rusty standing in a primitive kitchen stirring something in a skillet.

"Coffee?" he said.

"Uh...yes...please." I started to move but then remembered my nakedness. Even though he'd taken my clothes off last night, I didn't want to wander round without them in the daytime, but I couldn't see them anywhere. He must have seen me looking because when he brought me coffee he said, "They're in the launderette. I went in early so no-one would see me washing a woman's clothes." He blushed again. "I'll go fetch them in a few minutes."

The coffee was great. I sat up in the bed with the sheet pulled up until Rusty pushed a plate of eggs and bacon at me. I stuffed my face for a minute before I looked up at him.

"Why?"

"Why are you here or why I am helping you?"

I nodded, meaning both, my mouth full again.

"My Pa, that's Dan that you met yesterday, sold you the car. Over dinner he told us what a deal he'd made. Probably make a hundred out it," he said, "and he cackled about how you'd chosen the worst piece of junk on the lot. When you came in for gas I recognized it and knew he'd finally suckered someone. I was going to tell you but then old Fatso came out..."

I smiled. "You could have told me when I arrived."

"Well, I was real nervous, you being such a nice lady with a beautiful smile. When I went to help you with the hood release I was shaking so much..."

I couldn't help teasing him. "I know. Your arm had brushed my thigh."

He sat down on the bed his eyes like saucers.

"It's no big deal, Rusty."

He looked straight at me. "I know, but still." He averted his gaze. "I bet Fatso bad mouthed me, huh?"

"He did say you made a habit of cozying up too much with the lady customers."

"Hey."

I'd offended him again and said, "Sorry."

"He's been on my case ever since that Janice came in and waggled..." More saucers. "I can't believe I said that."

"It's okay," I said, keeping my voice low and sympathetic. "I was a teenager once."

"Well, I do enjoy flirting with the ladies and a lot come to our station because Mr. Frosty at the Exxon up the road is a real old grump. Usually I'm shy until they've been in a few times and I get to know them better."

"Pretty good job to meet the girls?"

"Yeah. But they usually come in with their boyfriends and they just treat me like a grease monkey. Anyway I watched you from the office window and as you drove away I saw the drips of oil you left behind. So after dinner when Pa was still gloating I thought I should go check you were okay."

"That was kind of you, Rusty. I appreciate it."

"You should have seen all those parts scattered down the road. Is that why Tom stopped?"

"He wanted to know if I needed help, but then he had a call." I lay back down and made sure the covers were well pulled up. "So where are we now?"

He laughed. "We're in my apartment, well it's more like a shed, that Pa gave me when I threatened to move away."

I looked round. The double bed filled this room with a foot to spare and the little kitchen was beyond the sheet in the doorway.

"Rusty, is there a bathroom?"

"Oh yes, of course. Come on through here and I'll show you." I let the sheet drop partway down my breasts and he blushed. "Let me find you something to wear."

"I'll just wrap this sheet round me, Rusty. And do you have a shower?"

Ten minutes later I walked back into the bedroom shivering. A shower yes, but hot water, no. He'd laid out my clothes for me, not ironed but washed and clean. He waited just through the kitchen in the other small room which seemed to be a large hallway with the entrance door in the far wall. He was sitting on a small couch when I went through.

I smiled at him and you'd have thought he'd just

got tickets for the World Series. Then I looked out of the small dirty window and gasped.

"You didn't tell me we were here." I was looking at the back of the car lot; the one where I'd bought the car. I worked at keeping my voice real cool and said, "Rusty, does your Pa come visit you often?"

"Nah. He thinks it's a dump. But by giving me some freedom he figures I'll stick around and learn the car business. He wants me to take over here sometime."

"So why are you working in the garage?"

"That's temporary until business picks up here. He thinks I'll learn some mechanics at the garage, like free training. Fat chance. Anyway, we worked out this deal. I stay around and he gives me this place, with a key an'all. That way my music doesn't annoy him."

I looked around. No radio, no TV, not even a Dansette record player.

He saw my puzzled look and reached behind the little couch. "Pa hates the noise I make with this." He waved a black case and took out a fiddle.

"You play?" What a dumb question. He took the bow out of the case and played for twenty minutes. I sat transfixed. "You sure know country," I said. "How long have you been learning, Rusty?"

His eyes were shining brightly and his nerves and shyness seemed to have evaporated. "Mom made me have lessons for four years," he said, "She insisted."

"Good for her," I said. "That was great. You know anything else?"

He treated me to another country tune and as I tapped my feet he looked over and smiled.

He put down the fiddle. "I have to go to work now.

I'm on the afternoon and evening shifts. There's food in the fridge and I'll be back around nine, if you're still here?"

"Rusty, I'm exhausted and if it's okay with you, I will hang around for a bit."

He smiled and said, "That's great, but don't let anyone see you in here. Pa would wonder what's going on and people might think…" He blushed again.

I tried not to smile. "I'm going to need your help to get out of here, Rusty, so I'll wait for you till tonight. Thanks so much." I leaned forward and kissed him.

Puppy dog eyes again. He almost ran out the door.

Colt sat and looked at me with, I think, approval in his eyes.

The Woman on the Knoll

Seventeen

The little cabin was noisy all day. Half of the back lot of Dan's Autos was a Pick'n'Pay junk yard and people wrestled with the wrecks till they found the part they needed. Periodically Dan used an old forklift to shift the towers of debris to give access to other vehicles, or to add more to the piles. My Ford came in around 4 pm.

I spent an uncomfortable afternoon, alternately waiting for a dreaded knock on the door, or replaying the last weeks in my mind. I nibbled on some cheese and crackers then took refuge in bed, falling asleep to the crack of rifle fire, the sound of screams and shouts, and the pink suit.

Colt must have jumped on the bed at some point because I woke up with slobber on my face. I dozed again. Later, still muzzy, I struggled with the covers and woke up to a noise.

"Hey," Rusty said, "here's a drink." He flicked on the bedroom light and came in.

I sat up and grabbed the can of Coke, then had a brief moment of panic until I remembered I'd slept in my t-shirt. He grinned at me, went back into the little kitchen and came back with a bag of food. I opened it, one burger and fries. I looked up.

"I already ate," he said. "I get a break early evening to have dinner. And I couldn't have gone to the drive through and picked up two orders without everybody knowing and wondering why."

Burger juice dripped down my chin as he talked. The fries were okay, but a bit soggy. I coughed on the bubbles in the Coke.

"Some visitors came into town this afternoon," he said. "They were looking for you."

I froze, a fry halfway to my mouth. How could they have tracked me down so fast?

"They saw your old car on the lot here and asked Pa about you. Then they came to the garage and I gassed up their Chevy. Luckily Fatso hadn't towed the Ford back yet. They left their car at the pump and one of the guys, there were three of them all wearing suits, went across to the office and talked with Fatso for a long time. Then old Mrs. Cary drove in with her Dodge and I gassed her up. I was washing the windshield when Fatso came out and called me over. Mrs. Cary got angry because her windshield got streaked since the sun was full on it. I went in the office and told him Mrs. Cary was getting pissed. 'The heck with Mrs. Cary,' he said, 'Mr. Bronson here's got a few questions for you.'

"I looked at him, all expensive suit, town shoes and Straw boater and since I'd seen some episodes of Dragnet I said 'what are you, FBI?'. He just laughed and said 'Here's my I/D.' He leaned forward to shake my hand and left me clutching a dollar bill. He asked me about gassing up the Ford, and then about you. I said, 'You mean the one with the pretty face?'."

I couldn't help but smile when he said that. Rusty was my one ray of sunshine.

"So I told him how I gave you full service, stroked your leg and got my face slapped. They all laughed but I thought if I told them I'd made a fool of myself they'd probably leave me alone. And it worked. They just asked where you were going so I said towards Woodfield. They nodded like I'd said the right thing and gave Fatso five bucks. Then they took off. What do they want you for?"

Good question. I should have anticipated it and my mind blanked. "Tell you later," I said. "Did you see them again?"

He shook his head. "They never paid for their gas either. Fatso was real pissed about that. He said it was my fault but I'd had to go calm down Mrs. Cary. She was real irritated and called me all kinds of names until her husband came along. Then she got all nice and friendly. The reverend paid and then they drove away." Rusty looked me in the eye and said, "Do you think I did right?"

I got up from the bed, went over to him and gave him a hug. He just stood there. "You did great Rusty." Then he put his arms around me and hugged back. Teenagers being, well, teenagers, I disentangled us when I felt something between us.

"What are we going to do?" he said.

"You're doing nothing, but I'm leaving tonight."

"You sure? Everybody in town's talking about you and you're bound to be seen."

He was right of course, and I was still exhausted. I nodded then realized he was staring at me. I'd forgotten I was only wearing a T-shirt and panties and grabbed my jeans. He turned away. I've no idea why. He'd seen a lot more before I started putting more clothes on. And he'd undressed me when he'd put me to bed the night before. He seemed relieved when I told him he could turn round.

We sat on the couch. I needed a friend and I think he needed one too. Small town life was getting to him. I told him all about of San Francisco and Santa Cruz with its boardwalk and roller coaster. The best they ever got in town here was a traveling fair. His eyes lit up when I mentioned the Golden Gate Bridge.

"I've never seen the ocean," he said.

Colt came and nuzzled in between us.

"He's a mutt," Rusty said, "but he's real intelligent. I got him from the pound."

I ruffled the fur between his ears and his eyes half-closed.

I had some ideas about getting away the next day but decided it was the wrong time to raise them. "How about some more fiddling?" I said.

He entertained me for the longest time before we got tired. When he put the violin down I told him he should join a band, go on the road, make a few dollars and see the world. He had a rueful smile on his face as I got up from the couch.

"That would be nice," he said, "but Pa needs me here."

I brushed my teeth over the dirty sink with his toothbrush. The taste was disgusting, but I still felt better after wards. I undressed in the bedroom and heard him scrabbling round in the outer room.

"What are you doing?"

"Making my bed."

"On the couch?"
"Yeah, that's where I slept last night."
'Were you comfortable?"
"It was okay," he said.
"If Colt lay down between us we could both sleep in here."
"No, I'm okay," he said.

I put out the light, climbed into bed, and must have fallen asleep instantly, even after I'd dozed most of the day. When the pink suit 'emerged' in my nightmare and woke me up, it was pitch black and I was shivering. No dog tonight. I pulled up the covers that had fallen on the floor then needed to pee. I got up and went through the kitchen to the freezing bathroom. Coming back through the kitchen I tripped over the garbage can and it toppled over with a crash.

Colt was there immediately, with Rusty just behind. He grabbed my arm and said, "Are you alright?"
"Just cold," I said.

Colt licked my feet and Rusty led me back to the bedroom. I touched his hand and it was freezing too.

"Come on," I said. "Get into bed here with me."
He said, "That wouldn't be…"
"If you're worried, I'm not. And Colt's already on the bed."

I nestled down under the covers while the two of them sorted themselves out. I felt comforted by their presence even with the dog smell and snuffling.

"Rusty?"
"Yeah?" His voice sounded nervous and tight.
"Thanks again for everything."

He snored. I understood and smiled. Even now I

was warmer I couldn't sleep. I was distracted and I fidgeted. Colt growled softly at me and I poked him in the ribs to quiet him. He huffed and moved away, to the other side of Rusty, who shifted toward me. I felt his body close as he shuffled onto the warm spot Colt had left and I could tell his back was toward me.

My mind wandered to dangerous place. What was I thinking of? I wasn't thinking, that was the trouble, or maybe I was thinking too much. I needed to be held, comforted. He was only young, but he... I moved closer to him and gently spooned, feeling his warmth. I snuggled in and lay there, listening to the rhythm of his breathing. I felt Colt move off the bed. I sighed.

Rusty shifted and started to roll over my way. His breathing changed a little, but I could tell he wasn't awake yet. I rolled with him so that he was now spooning me. I felt his arm coming round my waist and then he stiffened. He'd woken and was probably about to freak out.

I whispered, "Rusty? Would you cuddle me, please?"

He stayed rigid for long seconds then started to relax. I moved my hand to his and pulled his arm more around me. We lay there in companionable warmth and fell asleep.

Finally at dawn, Colt came back up on the bed and squirreled in between us. I laughed for the first time in weeks.

That evening Rusty extracted a Dodge from a different part of the lot and brought it round to the cabin. He left it running and got out, face beaming. He was so proud of it even though it looked crap with a drooping rag top, and a paint job even worse than those little Honda imports I'd seen rusting away in San Francisco's salt air. I couldn't imagine what good it would do me.

He smiled at me in the dim light. "She's gassed up and ready to go."

I didn't have the heart to say anything.

He put his arm round my shoulders, pointed at the front of the car and gently pulled me forward. He lifted the hood and held it up for me to see the engine. Even in the twilight I could see the gleam of polished metal and clean new fittings, wires, and hoses.

"I was keeping the bodywork for last."

"I can't take it," I said. "You must have worked so hard on it. And your Pa will…"

"He doesn't know about this one. I'm always messing around with two or three of the wrecks and he gets a great deal out of it. He sells them and we split the profit fifty-fifty. He won't miss this one."

"But you will. You'll need this for prom nights and…"

"And now it's yours," he said.

I smiled and said, "Thanks," kissed him long and hard, then jumped in the driver's seat. "I'll let you know where I leave it," I said, and drove away.

Forty miles down the road, in the opposite direction from my first escape from the town, I stopped and barfed. Too much stress; I had to stop upchucking like this.

Eighteen

I was down to my last five dollars. The Rockies were sharp against the clear mountain air and I was freezing. The Dodge's heater worked but the flapping rag top didn't keep much of the warm air in.

I parked outside the City Library and waited until a woman with dark hair came out. When she walked past me I checked the sidewalks. Both ways looked clear. I pulled down the baseball cap that Rusty had given me, got out and followed the woman. She had lunch at a sandwich counter, chatted with a couple of patrons, and returned to the library. I followed her back, this time at a greater distance, not worried about losing her in the crowd, until she returned to the library.

Later that day I parked a hundred yards away from a large house in acres of landscaping. The woman from the library drove up in an Edsel Corsair and parked by the house. The huge rear fins of the convertible made it look like it could damn near take off. I spent three hours watching the road and seeing nothing. Then I drove off, grabbed some dinner and spent the night in the car.

The next day I was broke and freezing cold. The woman again left the library at lunchtime. I checked the street until she turned a corner and then walked after her. She was nowhere in sight. I scanned the whole shopping area but still couldn't see her. I smiled and walked a hundred yards down to a restaurant on the left. Fresh oysters were advertised in the window. Fresh oysters in Colorado? A thousand miles from the ocean? I shrugged and walked in.

The woman was in a rear corner booth looking apprehensive and excited all at once. I went up to her and said, "Hello Sis."

She almost knocked me over as she grabbed me in a huge hug, squealing and crying. I hugged back but squealing isn't my thing. When we sat at the table I saw her close up for the first time. She looked older and had more lines on her face than she should at thirty-two. She talked non-stop about hubby and the kids, but the longer she went on the more I sensed a problem.

I held a hand up, "Sis, what's wrong?" I felt weird. I'd come here to ask for help but she looked like a bus had hit her.

"I'm just so pleased to see you again. Where have you been all this time?"

I let it go. "After you got hitched and moved away..." I didn't mention the sniveling shit of an Air Force officer she'd married, "...I did my best to get along with Dad, but you know how he is. He always liked you better even when you failed one of his tests."

"God I hated those. Do you remember the cargo net on the assault course? I was dangling upside down for ten minutes before he let you come up and rescue me."

I smiled. I'd got into trouble afterward for not getting her down quickly enough. Never could win with the bastard.

"After you left he dumped me on Uncle Jed."

"What do you mean?" Sis said.

"Daddy was okay as long as we were both there, but when you left he started drinking a lot so Uncle Jed took over, just like he did when Daddy got posted to Israel. Remember we stayed behind with him and that nanny?"

Sis frowned. "You still haven't told me what you've been doing."

The server came up and we both ordered hot tea, a habit we'd picked up in England when Daddy was posted to Upper Heyford.

"And please make sure the water is boiling. I want to be able to scald my finger in it," Sis called after her. "I want it bubbling when it's added to the tea," Sis said to me.

"I know. I was there when the waiter in the Savoy told us." Sis often forgot that I'd witnessed many of her rites of passage. Like the time I'd seen her let Bobby Jones put his hand up her skirt. She'd been seeing him for months but he never came to the house. Daddy wouldn't allow us to see boys so we met them in stolen minutes and occasional hours. Sis had been secretive about Bobby so of course we all knew at school. He was a senior when Sis was a junior and she was totally awed by him. He was tall, she thought him handsome, and we all agreed that his car was cool. The afternoon she snuck out to see him his car was in the shop, so I watched them walking down Greenleaves Road. That sounds terrible, like I'd been watching my sister all our lives, but this was an exception. I knew something was up. They headed north toward the woods that backed up to the shooting range. All the kids at school knew it was the best place for making out. Most of their parents had

The Woman on the Knoll

probably used it when they were younger.

I followed them in advance by cutting through a horse ranch. The inner thicket was the preferred spot and I knew they'd head there. I had time to hide in cover of a few bushes. They came running into the thicket and before I could breathe, they were necking on the ground. Bobby moved on top of Sis and she had her arms tight round his neck, kissing him furiously. They rolled over and Bobby put his hand on her breast. She squirmed but didn't say no. Well she couldn't, the way she had her tongue down his throat. He whispered in her ear and she shook her head.

Silently I said, 'Go on, say yes'.

Sis's skirt rose higher above her knees as they made out on the grass, Bobby's hands grabbing at whichever breast he could reach. Sis slowed him down, opened the front of her blouse and let his hand explore inside. I guess that was why she hadn't worn a bra that day. They kissed some more and then he withdrew his hand and slid it down her thigh to the hem of her skirt. I heard her say, 'Mm mm' and she wriggled on her back. Bobby's hand disappeared up her skirt and she started writhing. I knew watching them was wrong, but I couldn't stop myself. I figured that as I knew about the birds and the bees I might as well catch up on people too.

Sis's knees came up and her face contorted just before she damn near flew up off the ground, her butt rising and falling. She stuffed a fist into her mouth and I could see she was silently screaming in pleasure. Bobby took his hand out from under her skirt. Sis lay there panting, and when she got her breath back, pushed him back against a tree. She got to her knees, opened his fly, and wriggled her hand around until she could pull him out.

Then she gave him a blow job, right there in the thicket, with him leaning back against the tree. I'd never seen an erect penis and it made quite an impression. I'd never told Sis what I saw that day, but two years later, when Sis had left home, I let Bobby go even further with me; in fact I chased him until he popped my cherry.

"Jan? Are you okay?"

I came back to the present. "You ever see Bobby Jones after you left school?"

Sis looked at me, open mouthed. "What? Where did that come from?"

"I dunno, I just had a flashback."

"He was a dork. I never gave him the time of day."

I was still thinking that one through when she looked straight at me in the way she'd always done when we were kids. "Tell me about the last five years."

She always knew when I had a problem or was in trouble, which with Daddy was pretty often. I was so exhausted and tense that I flinched.

"I left home after a final blow up with Daddy. He wanted me to join the Service. They'd started to take more women then, but no way was I going to push paper in an office or cook a thousand meals a day, so I headed for California. Daddy always told me my painting was a waste of time and I was no good at it, so I enrolled in Art School. I did okay for a while, but it was a heavy scene, a lot of alcohol, partying, drugs…"

Sis used her low secretive voice. "Like reefers?"

I smiled. "Yes, like reefers and a lot more besides. Eventually I realized I had an addictive personality and went to see the college shrink. He was no help but he did make a move on me."

The Woman on the Knoll

"Did you report him?"

"No point," I said. "I was a student with a head problem who went to a psychiatrist. Who would have believed my word against his? "

"Yeah…" Sis's eyes half closed and she pursed her mouth.

I was sure she was about to add some comment, but the moment passed.

"So what did you do?" she asked.

"I keyed his car."

"No. What happened to you after that?"

"I dropped out and traveled a bit round the southwest with a girlfriend until she discovered the man of her dreams and went off with him."

"Did they get married?"

My sister the puritan. "No, they didn't get married. They just shacked up together in the mountains somewhere near Tahoe. Last I heard they were doing well."

Liar. I hadn't been in touch with them in two years.

Sis groaned. "You've done so much and met such different people. All I did was get married."

"Sis, being on your own isn't the best place to be. Down in Mexico I met a dreamboat but after a couple weeks he let slip he was married. Another dead end relationship. So I ended up here today."

Sis knew, she always did. "No you didn't. You've missed out a whole bunch of stuff. Where did you go next and why didn't you call me in all that time?"

I licked my lips. I was getting increasingly uncomfortable with her questions.

"I couldn't call you because Daddy would have forced it out of you."

"No he wouldn't. He hasn't mentioned you in all the time since you left."

"So he must have had a real shock when I called him a few days ago. Disowned is the word that comes to mind. I never got as far as asking him for money."

Sis gave me the look again. "So you've only come to see me for money?"

"I'll admit that's part of it." I blustered some more about wanting to see her after so much time, but she pursed her mouth.

"You sure you want to know more?" I said.

She nodded.

"I settled in San Francisco for while but after a year of supporting a string of loser boyfriends I'd got through the trust fund Grandma left me."

"All of it?"

"Afraid so. I was pretty stupid."

"So how did you survive?"

I could tell from her tone that she disapproved of the hedonistic lifestyle but still found my story exciting.

"I moved to a smaller apartment and went on the streets. I made a living by…"

"What?" her exclamation was heard all down the restaurant. I couldn't have got a bigger reaction if I'd told her I was pregnant.

I laughed and continued. "…painting. What did you think?"

She blushed. I'd always been able to wind her up. "I always knew I'd end as a starving artist, and I did. The short story from then on is that I was saved by David."

My eyes watered and tears ran down my cheeks.

Sis leaned forward. She'd always been intrigued by

The Woman on the Knoll

my love life. Of course that worked both ways, for example, Bobby. "So this David...how did you meet him?"

"That part is really weird. We were shooting at the same gun club."

"You still shoot?"

If only you knew, Sister dear. "Yes, Daddy ingrained it in me. When I still had some money I got a membership in this gun club, and one day David was at the next station. We started chatting, you know, like you do when you're checking your target between sessions, and we ended up having a friendly competition. I beat him out of sight, he asked me out and soon we were going steady."

"Sounds like you were smitten."

I laughed. "Smitten? What a great word. Are you reading romance novels now?"

"As a matter of fact I am, if it's any of your business."

Oops. I'd upset her again. "Yes, I think we were smitten with each other, Sis, because I moved in with him. I continued painting but somehow it didn't seem so important and we traveled a lot for six months."

"How could you afford that?"

"Unlike me, David had money that he hadn't squandered."

"So are you two still together?"

I knew the question was coming but had prepared for it. "He died."

"I'm so sorry Jan; it must have been terrible for you."

The sympathy did it, plus the guilt I carried. The dam broke and I howled and sobbed. Later Sis told me that the whole restaurant looked over to see if I was either in pain or a lunatic. I've no idea how long it was before I quieted down. I remember Sis moving round the booth to hold me, but her sympathy that made me bawl even more.

After my outburst I would have preferred to sit outside to escape the fascinated gaze of the customers, but winter is cold when you're a mile high. We went back to Sis's house after she promised that Hubby wouldn't be home for hours. "Cheyenne Mountain is always in a state of quiet panic, but it's even worse with the death of JFK. John can't tell me much about what he does at NORAD, but it's obvious they're in crisis mode up there."

We settled down in her mountain log home, cozy by the fire and with a stiff drink. In my case a Jack Daniels, and for her, a strong tea.

"So how are you and Hubby getting on?"

She flashed me a look as if to say, 'Who says we aren't getting along?', but she must have needed to talk to someone because she said, and "I'm fed up with marriage and the sex I'm supposed to put out for him."

Wow. Sis never came out with stuff like that, never in the whole eighteen years we grew up together. I waited but she clammed up on me. Looked like we were both in deep do-do. I moved from my couch and sat by her. When I put my arm round her she burst into tears.

"Do you want to talk about it?"

"I've always hated sex, ever since..."

She went rigid in my arms and stopped speaking. I tried various ways to bring her back and in the end went for the jugular. "Who was it?" I asked, already knowing.

"Uncle Jed," Sis said.

I nodded.

"I was a virgin but Daddy wouldn't believe me

when I told him. Said he'd talked with Jed and believed him. There was nowhere to go for help so I kind of bailed. John asked and I married him. I always felt that I'd abandoned you when I left home so early. I was always scared for you too." She looked at me. "He didn't, did he?"

I wondered whether to tell her. I didn't want her to feel guilty but the truth always comes out. God, I hoped I'd be dead before all my past came out. I nodded and said, "He assaulted me too but I wasn't a virgin. You must have been traumatized."

"Sex has been horrible ever since. John thinks I'm frigid but I do try."

I hadn't wanted to just bum money off of Sis, but now I saw a way to help her in exchange. "Okay Sis, I need a couple of things. First some cash; you want to cut a deal?"

"You know I'll help you, Jan. We don't need to cut a deal."

"Yes we do. The way our trusts were set up it's going to be a pain for you to get money out at short notice. Bankers hate that kind of crap, but in return I'll get us revenge on Jed."

Sis looked me in the eye. As a kid she'd never been assertive and had always avoided confrontation so Dad had an easy time with her. The one time she'd held firm I recalled, was when she left home. Now I realized why; Uncle Jed. The bastard deserved to suffer.

"What do you say, Sis? We have a deal?"

"Of course. And like I said, the money is here for you anyway."

I grimaced. "You haven't heard how much yet."

"So tell me."

I halved the amount I'd been thinking of. "A

thousand dollars."

Sis blanched. "How much?"

"Sorry. I meant to say five hundred."

She looked down at the table. I could see the cogs whirring. "No you didn't, Jan, and I'll do what I can." She looked up at me. "How much trouble are you in?"

I'd been waiting for this too, but still hadn't come up with a brilliant answer.

"Are you in trouble with the police?"

Hah! If only. "Kind of, but not quite like that. David…" I thought back to his last anguished words and choked.

Sis's eyes teared up. "You poor thing."

"Yeah, well." Now I was getting emotional too, though I guess that would be normal for anyone whose boyfriend was tortured before she abandoned him to be killed. And now my sister was feeling sorry for me. I was about to bawl my eyes out again. No way would that happen, I was the tough sister.

"So?" she said.

"What?"

"You were telling me about your problem."

Shit. She was right. All that emotional stuff about David had blanked my brain. Couldn't afford to let that happen.

"David was working on a business deal when he died. He owed his partners two thousand dollars and they decided I should pay. I was lucky and got away."

"Could they follow you here?"

"No. I used a different name in San Francisco so they've no way of knowing about you." Unless they'd sweated it out of David.

"You don't look too sure."

Dammit. Must learn to keep a better poker face. "Yes I'm sure darling, anyway your married name is different, right?"

"So why would businessmen chase you? Wouldn't they go to a lawyer and sue?"

My big sister knew more about this world than I thought.

"There's more than you're telling me, Jan. David was mixed up in something else and these guys aren't exactly white as driven snow, yeah?"

I swallowed, wondering how little I could get away with telling her. "It wasn't exactly a business deal. David liked to gamble and he got involved with an illegal card club. When he was down by $500 he thought he'd keep going until his luck changed. At $2,000 they wanted their money. He didn't have it and then he died in a train accident."

"Oh God!"

I was trying to stay one step ahead of Sis's questioning and so far just managing. "He stepped into the path of a Southern Pacific train."

"Was it suicide or was he pushed?"

I couldn't believe it. She was soaking this up.

"Witnesses said he was on his own. But after that the casino heavies came after me so I ran."

I felt quite proud of this make-believe drama and Sis loved it.

"So where's Jed?" I asked. "Still at the same place?"

She nodded.

"And still active in the church?"

"Yeah, he's an Elder now and proud of it. Daddy's

always calling me and telling me what a pillar of the community he is. It makes me want to puke."

Nineteen

Jed's clinic was in the best part of town, just as I remembered it. At the back he'd improved the lock but it still fell apart when I figured out the best leverage for my pry bar. I went through to the little pharmacy and found what I wanted in a small cabinet secured with an even flimsier lock. I slipped the bottle into my pocket, along with a hypo. Then I plucked up the courage to go into the exam room. I just stood and looked, memories shrieking at me. This was for me as well as Sis. On the way out I called the cops.

I walked three blocks before I heard sirens. One mile up the road I came to Jed's house. I paused and looked up the driveway to the small mansion, all white stucco and stupid columns. A mock Greco temple in suburbia! What a crock. There were lights in a couple of windows and when I peered in through the gates I could see ruts where the gravel had been sprayed by a car accelerating hard. On the street a hint of burnt rubber hung in the air. I walked to the hedge near the gate and backed in into the shrubbery. Two hours later a car roared up the road, slammed on its brakes, and revved while the gates opened. Then it slalomed up the gravel and slid to a halt in front of the house. The driver went in and slammed the door.

As the gates were closing I eased through the gap and walked toward the house as if I owned it. He'd made it easy for me; a window was unlocked on the ground floor. I slid in and waited in the dark to make sure I hadn't been noticed. I crept into the hallway and saw light spilling through the door of a room ahead. When I reached the doorway I heard the familiar tones of Uncle Jed bellowing.

"Goddammit. I pay enough in premiums to get decent service from you guys. Get someone over there now and start figuring how much you owe me. Yes, the place is secure and boarded up. Yes the cops are keeping a close eye. Dammit, stop with the questions and get on this!"

I heard him slam down the phone and pad across the carpet. A bottle clinked against glass and a chair creaked. I waited through four more clinks and fifty minutes, and then watched as he staggered on the first step of the staircase. He leaned on the banister and fumbled his way up. A light came on and flooded the landing and I heard a door crash open. I waited another fifteen minutes then went up and found him laying face down on the bed, fully clothed. I walked round the bed and saw his face was more blotched than ever from the booze. He didn't smell much of alcohol. Must have been drinking vodka or gin. I smiled. Any kind of alcohol would make the job easier. I brought out the hypo, filled it, and jabbed him in the butt. This was the tricky part. I had to get him under without him seeing me. He squealed and jerked, then wriggled while I held him down. He almost threw me off but then gave an 'oomph' and lay still.

Ten minutes later I wished I'd gone for him outside. I was able to drag him along the floor and kind of roll him downstairs more or less under control, but getting him to the front door and into the car was a real pain. He was heavy and I had a hard time getting him into the passenger seat without him falling out. I finally squeezed him in and slammed the door. He rolled partway over into the driver seat.

I left him there and went back into the house with a box of matches.

He was leaning on my shoulder as I drove away and I chuckled at the sight of the porno magazines and photos I'd dropped all over the seats. I wondered who'd find them. I opened the gate with the remote on the visor and drove out. Looking back in the mirror I saw a flicker of flame and some smoke where I'd left the front door wide open. I waited a couple minutes until the fire was well established then drove downtown.

I drove two miles to the entry drive of the church and pointed the Caddie at the narrow gap between the stone walls. I squeezed it through, gashing each side of the car with wrenching noises of torn metal. Accelerating hard I aimed for the corner of the brick wall ahead of me and angled so that it hit on the front passenger side. The front crumpled as far as the engine compartment before it stopped. Jed was thrown against the windshield but his limp body didn't seem too damaged. I pulled him across to the driver's seat, got out and waited for a few minutes to make sure the car didn't catch fire. When I heard vehicles approaching I took off round the building and ran through the cemetery. I jumped a low wall and fell into the side of a car. I crashed to the ground and felt a hand on my collar.

I flailed around in the dark until Sis said, "Stand up you idiot and get in the car."

I was giggling like a maniac as she helped me up. She slapped me across the face.

"That's rude, Sis. What would Hubby say if ..."

Slap! She did it again. "Ow!" But it was enough to unscramble my brains and drag me down from the euphoric high.

The Edsel flew out from behind St. Patrick's Catholic Church.

Poor Jed.

The Woman on the Knoll

Twenty

The tide rolled up Frenchman's Bay stirring the lobster pot buoys. In the distance I could see Mount Desert Island and Cadillac Mountain shining in the morning sun. Mid-summer had arrived. I loved cycling to work at this time of year after so many winter months of cold and ice. The bakery was a warm haven at the end of the ride and the smell of the dough and yeast always welcomed and mellowed me.

The weather had been cruel during my first northern winter. When I arrived in the fall I found a small cottage at a rent I could afford and had been welcomed into the small family running the local bakery. The pay covered my rent and necessities; just what I needed to lay low and recover. In the last five years I'd lived in six states in trailer parks, flop houses and apartments. I hadn't stayed anywhere for more than a few months, either because my neighbors were weird or suspicious of me, or, as happened twice, I felt eyes following me. Whenever I felt that tickling down my spine, my body telling me I was in danger, I fled. Finally, here in Maine, I felt secure.

My cottage was almost perfect except I got through four cords of wood the previous winter keeping the cold at bay. I had a living room that took up half of the building and a small bedroom, kitchen, and bathroom. When it was below zero and the heat of the wood stove didn't reach the other rooms, I slept on the couch and got up in the middle of the night to stoke the fire. The nights I couldn't get to sleep I'd go to my rickety 'boards on bricks' bookcase and read some fiction. Often it was the Warren Commission Report.

After almost a year I felt that the small population was accepting me and I'd even helped on a lobster boat, hauling and re-baiting the pots. I'd never realized that live lobsters were a blue-black color and not red. The nearest town with a Police Department was twenty miles away and we only saw the occasional deputy driving through. That suited me fine.

The weather changed fast by the ocean here, and rain was falling hard as I steered my bicycle into the alley alongside the Bakkerie and parked it in the one dry spot under the eaves. I hurried round the back and rushed in through the stable door, although the two parts were bolted together when it was this cool in the morning.

The bakery was owned by a Swedish couple, Anna and Dagmar Flemel, and their daughter Lisl. The business premises wouldn't be allowed today with all the fussy hygiene laws, but we turned out great bread and baked goods. No one got sick from our products and who cared about permits. We were busiest in summer but had just enough trade from local towns to keep going year round.

As I went in I was assailed by the friendly smells of cinnamon, yeast, bread dough and sweet rolls steaming and cooking. If the pointing between the bricks in the walls was falling apart and the roof leaked some in the rain, who

The Woman on the Knoll

cared?

"Hi Lisl. Beautiful summer day isn't it?" I said as I adjusted the position of a bucket under a leak with a sneaky kick.

She looked up from the dough weighing machine and smiled. "Hi Jan, you're early."

I envied Lisl her long blonde hair, and not just because it was so gorgeous and so obviously not out of bottle, but because the tresses fell naturally over her shoulders and she never had dandruff.

I looked over at Lisl's mother. "Anything special this morning, Anna?"

She looked up from the counter top as she frosted cakes. "Just the usual, Jan, except we also have a rush order for 300 dognuts for the Fireman's Annual Festival."

"Dognuts?"

"Same as doughnuts but twice the frosting. Can you handle that?"

"Sure." I started weighing out the flour.

"What's the festival?"

"It's been a local tradition for ten years, ever since Billy Maddox was killed here," said Anna.

Lisl blinked. A tear fell into the dough on the scales. She said, "He was a volunteer firefighter and he should have been sitting in the rumble seat but he fell as they turned this corner. Stupid really, because it was a false alarm. So they had the first Festival in remembrance of him and to raise money for his family. That was a waste of time. His Mom drank it all away and died 18 months later. Some called it from grief, others from alcoholism. The party is still called the Festival rather than a Roast or just the Fireman's Barbeque, but now the money raised goes toward the Community Center. I don't know why I'm telling you all this, Jan, it's ancient history..."

Anna had told me before that Lisl had been going steady with Billy, but I hadn't realized he'd been killed just outside. "Must have been hard on you, Lisl."

She ignored my comment and continued. "It's always at the Fairgrounds. Everyone brings cakes or cookies to raise money and we always do a large batch of dognuts."

"Why are they called dognuts?" I said.

Lisl smiled. "Years ago, Fred, one of the locals, he's dead now, was drunk and he fell over a lawn chair and hit his head on the corner of the baked goods table. The doughnuts spilled on to the grass and within ten seconds there must have been a dozen dogs fighting over them. So ever since then - dognuts."

Three hours later it had stopped raining and we delivered the dognuts to the Firemens booth.

We also had leftover cookies and cakes which we donated to the Womens Club table. Lisl had objected when I suggested doing it but I knew it was only because Brian's Mom volunteered there. Lisl had been lusting after Brian for months but he usually had some out-of-town girl hanging off his arm. He was the owner of the small market just down Main Street from the Bakkerie, a broccoli to batteries, oatmeal to oranges operation, a little of everything but not much of any one. A fun little store when you found what you wanted. Lisl saw Brian every month at the Chamber of Commerce meeting and she got on fine dealing with him there but she came over all flustered and shy on a more personal level.

'Aw stoppit, Jan. Never mind your matchmaking,

but we could take the leftovers."

The fairgrounds were like many others in small town America. There was a tree shaded lawn and a stage set up at one end for the music acts, speeches, and prize presentations.

The grass in front of the stage was already flattened by dancers' feet and unusually for a summer dance, there was no dust; the rain had damped it down. The entertainment stalls and food tables were lined in a horseshoe facing the stage, with the bars set up at each end. The organizers knew from experience that dancing and beer feed on each other.

Lisl and I carried the boxes from the van to the baked goods table. I saw her face redden as we approached. Brian was talking to his Mom and smiled as we dumped the boxes.

"Hi Lisl, Jan."

His Mom said, "You're too good to us Lisl. We'll sell every one of these."

"Even if they're stale," Brian said, trying a feeble joke.

I smiled and Lisl flushed even more. Brian's Mom noticed. She nodded at me and I winked back as we shared the same conspiratorial thought.

"OK, Brian," I said, as the band started 'Lady Madonna', "What about a dance?"

He looked at me a bit weird. We'd hardly spoken before and now this upstart newcomer was in his face? Before he could protest I grabbed his hand and dragged him through the crowd. Over my shoulder I waved to Lisl to follow. On the dance floor the three of us gyrated to this latest Beatles hit, and then to the older 'Hello, Goodbye.'

Two more fast numbers followed before a slow dance started. I pleaded thirst and pushed Lisl and Brian together. They looked at me as if I were the devil incarnate as they realized my matchmaking, but I grabbed both their butts by the nearest cheek and pushed them closer. Brian's was nice and firm! As they bumped they were forced look at each other rather than me. I saw them holding each other tentatively as I left.

I circulated through the crowd ending near the bar. A glass of wine was calling me and I plunked down my 25 cents. The white was so chilled that it tasted acid.

I groaned as I heard a drunken voice to my right.

"Hey, bartender. This wine's sour. Don't you have any that's drinkable?"

He was two places down the bar from me. The woman with him pulled on his arm, shushing him, lines radiating from the corners of her eyes and creasing her forehead. "Ray, please. Don't make a fuss. These are my friends and neighbors."

He growled at her, and said, "You really enjoy living in this one horse town?"

I froze. I couldn't breathe and my vision blurred but I managed to turn my head away before either of them noticed me staring. I flushed then felt as cold as ice. I chugged a mouthful of my vinegary wine. I guess he had a genuine complaint, just like the time he'd bitched at Lee during the practice at the shooting range back in the fall of '63. Back then I'd avoided getting dragged into the argument, something to do with rifle sights, but the sound of their voices, Lee's high pitched and whiney, versus Ray's loud-mouthing, had stayed with me.

I dragged my ass off the stool, turned to walk

The Woman on the Knoll

away, and walked straight into Lisl and Brian.

"Hey! Where are you going Jan? We figured we'd buy you a glass of wine."

The last thing I wanted. I assumed Ray being here was some horrible coincidence, but he was way too close and I had to get away before he saw me.

Behind me I heard the woman say, "Come on, Ray. Let's head home."

Poor woman.

"What's so fascinating?" Lisl said. "It's just Patty's brother drunk again. I feel sorry for her, she's had enough pain in her life."

Some fancy fiddle work announced a new band on stage, bouncing somewhere between country and folk.

"Patty?"

"Yeah. Her husband Dan was drowned when his fishing boat sank. There was thick fog, he collided with the ferry and they never found his body. Her brother Ray comes up here maybe twice a year. They're so different you would never think they were siblings. She's sweet as pie, but Ray likes his booze too much. He's a mean drunk and last year he started a fight at the dance."

I watched as Patty led Ray through the crowd toward the parking lot.

"Where does she live?" I said to Lisl.

She laughed at me. "Why? You don't fancy Ray, do you?"

"Don't be silly," I said, my voice tailing off as I realized how I was becoming more suspicious of the coincidence. I had decided to follow him. If he was here with any of Tony's people, I wanted to know about it. I moved away from Lisl.

"Jan? Where are you going? The party's just got started."

"Humor me, Lisl. I'll be right back."

As I followed I noticed that Ray dragged his right foot. That was the clincher. Lee had mentioned that Ray had one leg shorter than the other, the result of a shooting accident. I'd never believed the accident part. They went round the corner of the stage, crossed the parking lot and got in a battered old Ford pick-up. As Patty turned it in the parking lot I got a good look at Ray and saw he was missing part of his right earlobe. That was the final clincher – I remembered noticing that at the range.

The band on stage was called Eddie and the Reddies, an awful name even for the sixties. They had a drummer, two guitars, a fiddle player and a singer. As I looked up the fiddle player was sitting taking a break during the guitarist's big solo. Suddenly he jumped off the stage right by me and shouted, "Jan?"

I swear I jumped a foot and was about to run when he said, "Don't you remember? I sure do." He smiled and said, "Your car broke down, my little cabin, I rescued you. You told me I should join a band. So guess what…?"

Of course. Young Rusty who'd hidden me for a couple of days when I was first on the run. He wasn't as young anymore, but he was still gorgeous. His eyes were the same deep blue but his halo of golden hair was even bigger now. He was ahead of the Afro style by years.

"What are you doing here?" we said to each other, and laughed.

"You first," I said.

"I formed the band about a year ago and we've been following the sun since then. South in winter and north in summer. This gig just kind of found us. What about you?"

Tricky one. "Sorry but I don't have time now, Rusty. Can we catch up later? Where are you staying?"

I had no intention of us getting together. This whole afternoon was turning surreal and however much I'd liked him, he reminded me of why I was in Maine. I couldn't involve him again. I turned to leave but then saw I Patty's truck was back in the parking lot and Ray was heading toward me. Shit!

Rusty was just saying, "The Motel 6 just up…" when I flung myself on him and stuck my tongue down his throat. He clung to me, shocked for a second, but then he gave back as good as he got. This tiger wasn't the same as the innocent that I'd shared a bed with five years before and I reckoned he'd been getting plenty of practice on the road.

When we came up for air he said, "Not that I didn't enjoy that, but why d'you come on so strong?" His eyes twinkled. "Couldn't resist me, huh?"

"Yeah, just couldn't not do it." I looked round to make sure that Ray, who'd come back around the stage and picked up a hat from the bar, had now left for good.

I sighed.

"What?" Rusty asked.

"I'm just so pleased to see you after all this time. Your dad still selling death traps?"

"No. He had a heart attack two years back and he left me the business. While I'm touring with the band my cousin's looking after it. God knows what kind of mess I'll find when I get back."

"And what about Colt?"

"I've still got him. He's in the bus just now. And guess what? I finally saw the ocean."

His familiar smile, starting at his eyes and moving down his face, creased his cheeks.

"So you like life on the road?"

"Sure. And before I forget I did get my car back after you called. Thanks."

"I'm sorry you had to wait so long. It took me a while to get my life back together." Like that would ever happen.

He smiled at me. "So why are we standing here talking when we could be picking up where we left off five years ago?"

He grabbed me by the arm and I realized there was no way he could have realized that my bodily assault and intense smooch with him was for my own selfish good, but as he pulled at me I also realized that he was a damn good kisser. The way I was now feeling, after years of celibacy, he could have had me right then and there in public, but a huge guy came along, grabbed him and damn near threw him up on the stage. "You missed your cue, Rusty. Get with it, will ya?"

His solo fiddle music drifted over the crowd as I crept back across the dance floor.

Lisl was deep in conversation with Brian when I found her. I could barely get her attention through the smoke of her 'herbal cigarette'.

"Lisl, can I borrow the van, please?"

She produced the keys from somewhere and rasped in a gruff voice, "Sure, and can you get me some munchies?"

"If you'll tell me where Patty lives," I shouted over

the music. I grabbed a handful of cookies from the table behind me and thrust them toward her.

"Lisl?"

She pulled back from Brian. "The cottage about two miles north of the harbor."

I grabbed the keys and went for the van. I took the long way around town to come at Patty's cottage from the far side. Her car was parked nearby and I saw her and Ray come out of the back door. Ray had a bottle in his hand and was heading for the rocker on the porch. If he was going to get on the outside of the bottle of Jack Daniels he was carrying, I figured he wouldn't be leaving that night.

I drove home and crashed, falling on my bed with a wild set of ideas floating in my head. When I'm in that kind of mood I know that I'm likely to wake up with some idiotic plan.

Twenty-one

I slept through my alarm. It was light when I got up and I staggered through my morning rituals. I clutched a mug of coffee and sat in the window seat watching the world go by, mainly gulls and rain. I showered, and drove around town again to Patty's cottage, but this time I pulled onto a nearby dirt road. The van was concealed from view but I could see her place through the tree branches. I turned on the radio, just getting the end of 'My Cabin Love' by Eddie and the Reddies. I was still laughing when the news came on and the world stopped turning for the second time in my life.

Robert Kennedy had been shot.

He'd been surrounded by a mob of supporters in the Ambassador Hotel in Los Angeles just after winning the California Democratic primary in his race for the candidacy for US president when Sirhan Sirhan had come up and shot him. It seemed cut and dried but the Warren Commission had said that about JFK's assassination too. I sat there in a daze, shaken to the core.

When I finally looked across at the cottage, one of the cars was gone. I couldn't care less.

Bobby had been shot three times at close range and

The Woman on the Knoll

was in critical condition. The hospital spokesman was not optimistic. I drove home listening to non-stop news reports that gave no new information. Then I saw Ray's car pass in the opposite direction, presumably on his way back to his sister's cabin. So what, I thought. I parked outside my cottage, went in, and tripped over the coat stand which was lying across the hallway. I looked up from the floor to see all my furniture, clothes, and other possessions scattered across the room.

My first thought was Ray. My second was my cache of identities. I had a false passport and two driver's licenses from different states. If I lost those I was in real trouble. I rushed into the bathroom and pried up a floor tile in the corner behind the door. The documents were all still there. With a sigh of relief I grabbed them and my clothes and packed a duffel. I added a few of the items I'd gathered over the years. The rest Lisl could have because I didn't think I'd be returning to Maine. What next? I couldn't think straight so I drove to the Bakkerie. I walked in and they all looked at me, faces pale.

I said, "You guys heard?"

They all nodded and Anna said, "Yeah. And with Martin Luther King still warm in his grave."

There wasn't much else to say. Lisl had brought a television into the kitchen and we all gathered round it. Later that day we heard Bobby Kennedy had died.

"That poor family," Lisl said. "That's three of the brothers dead now."

"Three?" said Anna.

"Yes. The eldest, Joe, was killed in World War II."

"I didn't know that," Anna said, and we all lapsed into silence.

The more news that came in about Sirhan Sirhan and his supposed connections with the Palestinian secret service, the more unlikely the official version seemed to be. Again the media had swallowed the immediate reaction that a single unbalanced gunman had killed a Kennedy brother. I wasn't sure. I thought it seemed more like another patsy set up by a conspiracy. But as more details emerged that afternoon all the eye-witness and photo evidence seemed to fit the lone gunman theory.

My brain started whirring on the more immediate issue of Ray. "I've had enough for one day," I said to everybody. "I'm going to run some chores. Can I keep the van for a while, Lisl?"

"You sure you have to go?"

I was having a hard time lying to her. "Yeah."

She looked at me with her head tilted to one side. "Okay."

I left, wondering if I'd ever see them again. Ray had been suspicious enough to turn my house over and had probably already told Tony that I lived in Weirhaven. I had no choice but to leave.

The only road out of town crosses what everyone calls the singing bridge, which makes an eerie thrumming sound as you drive over its metal grid roadway. Twenty miles down the road I waited at a rest stop with plenty of tree cover figuring that Ray would be less likely to notice me than if I followed him all the way from town.

He was a long time coming. After two his dark red Mustang came by and I tucked in behind five other cars. Even then I worried that he'd notice the distinctive Bakkerie paint job on the van but luckily the sides had taken the brunt of Lisl's artistry. As it got dark I crept up to

The Woman on the Knoll

within three vehicles of the Mustang so I wouldn't lose him.

He kept driving through the night, making only one pee and gas stop. I almost lost him then, because I had to pee and gas up too, but couldn't do either until he'd headed away from the gas station. I figured I was four minutes behind him after my stop and he'd been averaging 60 mph. If I drove at 70 I should catch up with him in 24 minutes. He must have been driving more slowly because I saw his car's distinctive shape with its missing tail light after 15 minutes.

We covered another 250 miles before he pulled over at a motel. When I saw him turn in and stop outside the office I drove by to scope out the area. The neighborhood was kind of funky but it seemed safe enough to leave the van parked on the street. I left it three blocks away in a piece of recent suburbia, all three bedroom and two bath ranch style tract homes. Ray wouldn't see it unless he cruised the neighborhood for fun. I walked back to the motel with a scarf on my head and saw that his car was parked by room 13. I figured that he'd either be in his room or having dinner at the 24 hour Denny's across the road, so I should be safe to check in. The lobby was stark but functional; all naugahide and sticky linoleum. The clerk was bored and listening to his transistor radio, tuned to some pop station with the stupid 'Henerry the Eighth' blasting out. He reduced the volume as he saw me coming and if it wasn't a snarl of annoyance then at least a grimace crossed his face.

"Yeah?"

"Yeah," I echoed back. "One room, one night," I said.

"Okay. Five bucks."

"And I want a room in the block across the way, facing the lobby."

"What for? You wanna watch your old man having a fling with a younger girl?"

I almost smacked his face, but I needed to stay as anonymous as possible.

"Cos the only new guy tonight was on his own," he chuckled, "unless she's coming later." He laughed some more at his own joke and I smiled bleakly. He gave me a key and said, "Room 21, just down there."

I put the five dollars down plus the 40 cents that I assumed would cover the local taxes, grabbed the key, turned away, and opened the door.

"Hey. You've got a nickel change.

"Keep it for your penny jar," I said and stepped out. I reached the sanctuary of my room without seeing Ray and gobbled down some of the cookies I'd bought in the gas station. With tap water they made a poor dinner, but I couldn't risk going out and being seen.

He got back at ten and I stayed awake till two am watching his door. At seven the next morning I resumed my vigil. He came out of his room at 8:30 and walked toward Denny's. I was starving and ate the last cookie before taking the stairs down to the first floor. In the distance I saw the maid pushing her cart toward the room just along from his. I went to his door and turned the sign from 'Do not disturb' to 'Please clean me' and then headed toward the maid. She was of Latino descent and I hoped her English was better than most of the maids in this country. She looked up and smiled.

"Hi," I said, "I'm just going for breakfast, but if you

could clean my room now that would be great."

She nodded, said "Si, Si," and pushed the cart up to room 15.

I sighed. "No, can you clean Room 13, please?"

"Que?"

"13, please."

"Ah...13," she said, and then pushed the cart along the cracked concrete. I watched her till she reached the right room then walked towards Denny's. I paused part way there, grabbed my stomach theatrically, and walked back to Ray's room. The door was open and the maid was emptying the trash cans.

"Excuse me," I said, still holding my stomach, "Could you come clean later? I think I have the stomach flu." I made the universal sign for being sick, opening my mouth and using my palm to mimic throwing up. She understood immediately and was backing out of the door before I needed to act out any more upchucking.

I was going through Ray's case before she'd closed the door. I didn't know much about the art of concealment, but I'd seen the newest James Bond movie and knew about false suitcase bottoms and secret compartments. I couldn't find anything like that but I did find a pistol tucked in among his socks at the bottom of the case. Semiautomatics were not my favorite weapon. Dad had many faults, but not teaching his daughters about the unreliability of pistols was not one of them. I had just moved to the closet where he had a suit and an overcoat hung up when I heard a key jiggling in the door lock. Of course it couldn't turn the way he expected and came open when he just tried the handle. Ray saw me straightaway and laughed.

"Jan. You came to visit, how nice." He crossed the

room to his suitcase and felt for the pistol. His eyes widened but then his features relaxed as he found it. He pulled it out and chambered a round with an ominous click. I hadn't moved all this time, playing the 'girl caught in the act' part. He laughed loudly, more confident now that he was holding his gun.

"Find anything interesting, Jan?"

"Nothing much," I said.

"So why did you follow me in that ridiculous van."

I stayed quiet. There was nothing to say.

"Did you really think I wouldn't notice you, or wonder why I slowed down after gassing up? I wanted to let you catch up."

Crap. I thought I'd been so clever following him to the motel and then in fooling the maid to let me in his room. He was still smiling when I shot him in the shoulder with my twenty-two revolver. He hadn't seen it because my hand was hidden behind the coat in the closet. His arm jerked, he dropped his pistol on the bed, and clutched at his shoulder. Thanks Daddy, I thought. Ray stood still, blood squeezing out between his fingers.

"The neighbors will have heard that."

"Don't you believe it," I said. "This little peashooter is as quiet as they come, and besides, no one else is around. They've all left for the day."

He blanched and slumped onto a chair. "So what do you want?"

"Don't you know?"

He squeezed his hand more tightly on his shoulder. "I haven't a clue what you're talking about."

"Now you're annoying me, Ray. You're making me out to be stupid. That's not nice." Then I shot him again, in the fleshy part of his thigh.

When his howling stopped and was replaced by hard breathing and curses, I said, "Didn't your mother ever tell you not to use bad language in front of ladies?"

He looked at me, his face contorted in pain. "Show me a lady and I'll…"

I leveled the gun at him.

"No. Wait." His voice had gone up an octave. "What do you want?"

I stared at him until he wilted and looked away.

"I'm in pain here, lady, give me a break."

"Now I'm a lady now, huh? Is that what you think of me? Imagine a young woman coerced into an assassination conspiracy, her fiancé tortured and killed, a marriage denied, and 50 years of a happy shared life ruined. Are you getting the picture yet, buster? I'm no lady." I circled round the bed to pick up his pistol but then froze as I heard the room door open behind me.

A voice said, "Drop the gun!"

Aw crap!

I did.

Twenty-two

"Thank God you're here..."

Ray never got to finish his sentence. A shot came from behind me and the back of Ray's head exploded onto the wall behind him. Whatever the newcomer had fired, it wasn't silenced and the noise echoed round the room. I fell forward onto the bed, my ears so shocked that I couldn't hear a thing.

I felt a kick on my leg and looked over my shoulder at a stranger. He had thinning blond hair and a dark beard that looked fake on his thin chiseled face. His features were pinched and the sallow tan on his face made him look sick. The pistol he held looked huge and he grinned. He beckoned me to stand and in backing away from me he gave me one chance.

When I had shot Ray he had dropped his gun on the bed and I had fallen on it in shock when the stranger's gun went off. I pulled it from under me swung around and pulled the trigger. For an instant I worried that the safety might be on, but the kick that the 9mm gave confirmed otherwise.

Weasel face jerked backwards and fell against the wall behind him, his gun flying to one side. I sat on the bed

The Woman on the Knoll

wondering what the hell was happening.

"Who are you?"

Nothing.

"I'm no doctor but you've got a chest wound and you're losing a lot of blood."

"We almost got you," he said. "Ray was always impetuous and I'm not surprised you got the drop on him. But me? You're the first woman to..." He had a fit of coughing that spewed blood up through his mouth. Rich, red, arterial blood. He looked down at it on his chest. "You know," cough, "you're a loose end," cough, "and that one day we'll get you." Blood rolled down his chin and onto his shirt.

"Ray worked for you and he called you from the road," I said. "Probably when he stopped for gas. You got here in ten hours so you probably came from 500 miles away, assuming you didn't fly."

He looked serious, which taking his condition into account was pretty apt.

"You work for Tony? Or someone higher up?"

"Why should I tell you?" he said between coughs, splattering more blood over me.

"Remorse for all your sins?"

"So you're a priest now?" He wheezed, the sound awful to hear.

He slumped down the wall. I sat on the floor just far enough away to be out of reach. I hadn't survived this long to be caught out by more tricks from these guys.

"Who killed David? Was it Tony?"

"Who cares? He died hard. He yelled for you and screamed your name till the end. He thought you'd honor the bargain and come save him and when you didn't he died cursing you."

"I don't believe you."

Even I heard the quiver of doubt in my voice.

"Whatever," he said.

"Who's your boss?"

"You think I'm not my own man?"

"And who was Ray and why did you shoot him?" I thought if I kept pestering him with different questions I might confuse him as the blood leaked from his body.

Finally an answer. "He was a grunt we kept around for muscle. Nothing between the ears, but he could follow orders. He even got you to follow him so we could meet. But now he was a liability and knew too much."

"And me?"

"Doesn't matter now, does it? I came to kill you. I should have shot you straight away." He shrugged, as far as he could with the wound in his chest.

"So who sent you? Who do you work for?"

He beckoned me closer but I wasn't falling for that old trick. When he realized that this was truly the end, he cracked a smile and said, "CIA."

"That's impossible," I said. "You're not allowed to operate in the US."

His smile grew wider, and then he coughed and died.

I stood up. Now I stuck in the room with two bodies. No way was the CIA story true. He'd been my best chance to follow the trail back to whoever had organized the assassins, killed David, and set me and Lee up. I'd probably never get another go at it. But I now had confirmation that David was dead, and also that they were still hunting me. Probably always would be.

The Woman on the Knoll

A loud banging on the front door brought me back to the present. The noise of the second and third gunshots had been huge and the sounds had probably been heard in the office. The banging became a pounding as I opened the small bathroom window and squeezed my body through. I was two blocks away and almost at the van when I heard sirens approaching the motel.

Twenty-three

Sardines like no other I had tasted were sauteing in the open air kitchen of the restaurant behind me. But not the tinned miniature squashed mess that American supermarkets sell. These were the real thing, decent sized fish, six inches long, cooked whole, sizzling in island's aromatic olive oil. The locals loved them and so did the visiting tourists.

I breathed in, willing myself to stay and finish the picture, a watercolor of the harbor with its old stone breakwater, cobbled quays, and the 13th century fort guarding the harbor entrance. The painted fishing boats, gaudy in their primary colors but draped with old stinking black nets drying in the sun, added character to the green of the harbor water and the deep blue of the sea beyond. I breathed in again, almost tasting the sardines.

"That's pretty cool."

I looked sideways, seeing a typical American backpacker, all T-shirt, cutoffs, and thongs. I groaned. Another guy with a corny line.

"Want to buy it?" I asked without looking up. That usually scared them off. Daddy might be generous with Todd's or Wayne's allowance, they were always Todd or

Wayne or Randy, but their funds didn't usually stretch to watercolors.

"I'm not sure. Why don't we talk about it over lunch?"

This time I groaned out loud, still not looking up at him from my low canvas stool.

He didn't take the hint but instead bent low. "You know you love seafood."

"Have we met before?" I said, looking at his face for the first time.

He smiled. "No, because I'd remember."

"And why would that be?" I didn't let it show but his suntanned face bore just the kind of open featured expression that appealed to me. I realized too late that my answer had opened the door for him and groaned again.

"Because I'd lose my bet."

"What?"

"I told my friend over there that I knew you from California. Told him that we'd dated a couple of years ago."

I looked down at my palette and said, "Go away."

"I beg your pardon?"

At least he was polite. "I said go away. You're annoying me." I slid my brush the damp burnt sienna mix and added a mast to the farthest fishing boat in my painting. His shadow stayed in my vision as I bent over the palette again.

"I'm kind of nice when you get to know me."

"I don't doubt it but I have a painting to finish before lunch and another I've been asked to do of the fort today. I don't have time for this."

I didn't often get two commissions in a week and I

was determined not to disappoint the customers. My only income was from my paintings and I tried to sell them as I sat by the harbor working on my next picture. Meager was the word that largely described my financial state and my meals.

"Go away," I said. "You're annoying me."

"I only meant..." he started to say.

I flicked my brush at him and a blob of burnt sienna flew into his eye.

He recoiled, rubbing at his watery and reddening eye. He said nothing; not a grunt of pain, a surprised yelp, or even a Goddammit. Instead he sat down beside me, took the small glass of fresh water that I'd been about to use for the next brush rinse, and used it to flush his eye. I stared at him waiting for some reaction.

"Rob told me you were cool but not that you were this feisty."

"What did you say? Who's Rob?" I said quiet, trying to conceal the rush of fear I felt. My stomach churned as I held his gaze. "And who are you?"

But I knew they'd found me again. All my running had been a waste of time. And if they could track me down to even this little Adriatic island they could find me anywhere."

"Just a guy who's found you and..."

He got no further as my palette and painting hit his face. He fell back as I pushed past him and left him sprawling on the cobbles. I ran. Along past the open air restaurants, through the thin crowds that were gathering for lunch and into the narrow alleyways that backed away from the harbor. These weren't the dirty alleys of a US city, but cobbled and friendly, with washing hanging from lines suspended above, old men sitting in the sun playing checkers, and women gossiping in the shade. Small tavernas were opening and I ducked into the first one. The owner, Henri, an expatriate Frenchman who in his cups one night had hinted that he had similar reasons to mine for being for being on the island, started to welcome me and then stopped.

"What is wrong, Jan?"

I blurted some stupid story out to him about a mugger and pushed him back through the curtains into the small office. "Henri, I need help. There's a man who…"

"Hush Cheri, I have…"

I yelped as I looked behind him and saw Bobby Smith coming through the curtain.

"What…?" I said, and guess I must have blacked out. When I came to I was on the floor with Henri looking down at me, his face working and worrying, his hands dry washing. I realized my head was raised and I tried to bend my neck to look back.

"Help me up, Goddammit," I yelled.

"Okay," said a familiar voice.

"No…I…"

The next time I woke I was in my own bed in the small apartment I rented just up the alley from the taverna. The room was cool, I had a sheet over me, my head hurt and I must have groaned.

"You're okay, Jan. I'm here."

I turned my head and Bobby came into view.

"What…?" I heard myself say.

He grinned at me with that familiar corner curl of his lips. The expression that had made him the first love of my life. Sis had chased him till he caught her, but around me he'd always been shy. When I was in twelfth grade he'd waited on the sidewalk to talk to me. I saw him ahead of me and averted my eyes, hoping he'd say something. As I came alongside him he said, "Hi Jan."

I said something intelligent like, "Hi."

Sis had dumped him soon after the Greenleaves thicket incident and left home soon after. He stood there moving his feet nervously. I knew what he was going to say and I longed to hear it, but God, the timing was awful.

"Jan, I was wondering...would you come to the dance with me next week?"

God, I'd felt awful. Of course I wanted to go with him to the dance; I'd liked him from a distance for all of those months. But John had just asked me out on the same night and although I hadn't promised him, I felt I had to let him down before I could agree to go out with someone else.

I remembered opening my mouth and stammering something silly like "I... I... need to talk to someone..." I remember my voice tailing away in embarrassment. He nodded and said, "Okay. See you here tomorrow?"

I nodded, and went home in a blue funk. The next day I let John down gently and waited anxiously through afternoon lessons. Would he be there? Would he think I'd been a dork yesterday?

I walked along in the afternoon heat, sweating more than usual. Yes! There he was, leaning against a fence. I knew for the first time what a leaping heart was. I came closer and kept my eyes down. My friends had told me to act demure... I kept walking and... nothing... Not a word from him. My own mouth had been dry with anticipation, but nothing? What had happened? Why hadn't he said something? Why hadn't I? I went home and cried all night.

The Woman on the Knoll

Then it happened again. Not on the sidewalk going home from school but downtown. I was on the way to meet my girlfriends and he was standing at a bus stop. I was surprised to see him and looked ahead, wondering if he'd notice me. The strangest thing happened. He looked at me like he didn't know me. But I knew his eyes were following me. I wasn't going miss this chance. I turned and walked back to him, then saw his eyes open in recognition.

"Why didn't you say, Hi?"

A week later we were in the thicket down Greenleaves Road.

So what was he doing here?

Twenty-four

"Jan?"

"I don't believe it." Articulate, that's me. "What are you doing here, Bobby?"

"On vacation," he said, "with a friend. You met Brad down at the harbor."

Oh boy. Not a Wayne, a Randy, or a Todd, but a Brad. And I'd assaulted him. I lay back with a groan, then too embarrassed and confused, rolled off the bed. I couldn't take all this. "Please leave, Bobby."

"But Jan, you..."

"Go," I said.

"But I want to..."

"Please, Bobby."

He got and closed the door quietly behind him. I lay down again and slept.

I opened my apartment door around three. On the step were my easel, brushes, and paints, neatly arranged, with a scrap of paper on top weighted down by my water jar.

His note read, 'Sorry for the shock, Rob.'

Hmm, not Bobby, but Rob now. I felt my cheeks burn and must have looked at the small pile for thirty seconds before gathering my wits. The bag I used for carrying all my painting materials wasn't with my painting stuff so I went back into the apartment and fetched my tatty old canvas one, all covered in paint smears and one huge splotch of bird poop that had never come out despite multiple washings. I remembered the day it happened, five years before, when I was celebrating my first anniversary of arriving on the island. I'd been on the cliffs at the north-east corner and my hand was flying over the paper. The colors were flowing from my brush and I'd never felt so at one with a painting. The cliff top was golden with flowers and the sea so violet that my accurate rendering of it looked too artificial. The sailboats coming and going in the marina below gave me lots of action choices to liven the scene. Even the sailing groupies hanging around for a free ride to other islands or the mainland were wearing bright colors instead of the usual grubby T-shirts and cutoffs.

    I'd finished and was packing my gear into the bag when the shadow of an Armenian gull passed over me. I'd looked up just in time for a gob of poop to land in the corner of my eye, stinging like crazy. I'd grabbed my water bottle and the small sponge I used in my wet washes and dabbed my eye until the stinging had stopped. Then I'd finished packing, and holding the still wet painting carefully in one hand had walked the six kilometers back to town. I'd unpacked the bag before I noticed that the rest of the seagull poop had exploded down the side of it and dried in a horrible crust. Repeated washings never removed the stain.

    So I packed my art supplies in the old bag and walked the 400 meters into town, back to my favorite spot at the edge of the harbor. I set up my chair and arranged my art supplies in their usual places on the low harbor wall then took my water bottle to the harbor side cafe and filled it from the carafe on an outdoor table.

The owner, Santiago, dressed in the white baggy shirt and tight black trousers that worked magic on the female visitors, waved across the crowded tables. I winked at the couple eating at the table whose water I'd taken, said "Thanks," and wandered back to my spot, feeling their gaze fixed on my back. I did this every day I was painting here and loved the different reactions from the diners. The British pretended it never happened, the Germans growled, French and Italians complained but stayed seated and gabbled at each other. The Spanish called for a fresh carafe and Americans, thank God very few had discovered the island yet, would stand up and shout. But today's Americans hadn't moved.

I stretched a new sheet of 'Aqua 120 bond' on my board, fixing it in place with the Sellotape which was the only sticky tape I could find in the stores there. I had to waste an extra inch of border on each painting because the ugly stuff tore the paper when I tried to peel it off. I started the commission in pencil, sketching the scene, a classic of the harbor, fishing nets and boats, the old castle, and birds squabbling on the water.

"Okay Jan, what's going on?"

I knew he'd come over after I'd taken the water from his table instead of the nearest one I usually used. He and Brad had watched me wend my way through the tables but said nothing when I'd poured the water.

I blinked in the sun's glare as I looked up at him. "Why are you here, Bobby?"

He moved so his shadow was on my face. "I've

been looking for you," he said.

I froze, water dripping off my brush onto my bare leg. "What?" I forced my body's fight or flee response down into my stomach. What if the mob had sent him because he knew my face? What if he'd been forced to work for them like they'd done with my fiancé David?

He laughed, ending with a familiar chuckle. "Just joking, but it's a great coincidence. Mind if I sit down?"

He moved to the side and settled on the low harbor wall. I half turned away from the sun to face him.

"Your brush is dripping," he said.

I glanced down and felt the wet on my thigh. I grabbed a dry rag and wiped.

"What do you want?"

"Nothing,"

His voice had dropped in pitch as he replied, a husky resonant sound that I recalled from school, when I'd had my crush on him.

I struggled to keep my voice calm, but still came out with a half squeak.

"So why are you here?"

"Brad and I are taking a sabbatical."

His tanned face was just as I remembered it, smiling hazel eyes, the small scar under his left eye, a relic from a fly ball, and ears that stuck out just a little more than normal. His full beard was new to me and not as well manicured as his hair. I was beginning to feel a little more secure as I saw his posture relaxing. His shoulders lowered as he leaned back to take in the sun, and he smiled with a familiar crinkle of his lips.

I could feel a frown starting on my face. "So are you and he...um..."

He laughed, louder this time. "No, no... Just good friends who are between girls and felt like 'doing' Europe. We started in London, and then went to Paris, then West Berlin, but we got tired of damp cities and wanted some sun. This is the third island we've hopped across. How about you?"

How much to tell? I sensed being more guarded as I trotted out my usual spiel. "I came here to paint and I make a reasonable living off the tourists."

"Do you have a boyfriend or anything at the moment?"

I stared at him. He still seemed relaxed with his hands gently resting on the top of the harbor wall, his legs dangling, and head cocked to one side. A broad grin stretched his mouth and his lips opened to show expensively beautiful white teeth. He must have had them fixed because I definitely remembered a snaggletooth in there somewhere.

"Why?" I said. He was still in control of the situation but curiously I was getting more secure in the conversation until he said, "Will you marry me?" His smile had gone, replaced by an intense expression as he leaned forward.

Jeez! "Shouldn't we at least date again first?" I said.

The Woman on the Knoll

Twenty-five

My answer had popped out before I even realized what he'd said. What the hell was going on? He mumbled something, his face turned bright red, and he stood and walked away. I sat there in shock. What had just happened? I turned on my small stool and watched him walk back to his table at the restaurant. I assumed he said something to Brad, who looked up with a frown on his face. Rob left the table and walked along the sidewalk toward the downtown area. I sat there, in shock I guess, looking at Brad, who called the waiter, paid the bill, and then hurried after Rob. I considered following them, but it was all too weird.

I turned back to the familiar harbor scene and continued painting, my mind in a whirl. I was bored with painting the same old harbor scene but the buyer, a loud American in an even louder Hawaiian shirt, loved it. He had asked me to include the old Roman jetty even though I felt it would destroy the symmetry of the painting but his extra fifty dollars persuaded me and I'd promised to deliver it to his hotel that evening. All afternoon I sweated paint and tried to crowd out the day's weird events. The sun was hotter than usual and the tourist crowds thinned out. They usually sought cooler indoor pleasures visiting the fort or the monastery up on the mountain but the more foolhardy got lobster red snorkeling, para-sailing, or swimming. I'd fallen for those tempting delights early in my stay on the island and could still remember my blistered and scarlet face.

By six I was in the cool hallway leading to my apartment and salivating at the thought of the iced lemonade in the fridge. Coming in from the piercing sunlight I didn't see the figure on the top step. Then I saw that my apartment door was open behind the man silhouetted there. Not Rob again?

Then a familiar voice from the past said, "Hello Jan."

Oh God.

It was Tony. They'd found me!

Twenty-six

I heard a scrape of a shoe in the passage behind me and made an instant decision. Dad would have been proud of me. Another painting bit the dust as it flew towards the guy behind me, and my second best painting bag went behind into Tony's face. I followed through with my head into Tony's stomach while he was still flailing at the bag. He doubled over and fishy breath washed over me. I pushed him to one side and leaped into my apartment, slamming the door behind me.

The banging on my door started just as I locked it. I looked round to make sure there wasn't a third guy already in the room. There wasn't. Not one of their people anyway, and no one alive. But Bobby was laying on the kitchen floor, unmoving, a pool of blood around his head.

The banging got louder and splintering sounds came from behind me as the door suffered. No time to wait. Across the living room was the kitchen with an island counter. I ran around it, flung open the cupboard door below the sink and grabbed the straps of the blue day pack lurking there. There was a set of French doors to my right and leading with my shoulder I ran straight at the crack between the two doors and crashed through onto the stone patio. I leaped over the small terraces that sloped away from the apartment and down through a grove of olive trees. In the middle of the trees I paused to sling the pack on my back and then ran through the shade to a road a hundred yards further on. I jogged along the road to the right for fifty more yards then cut through a stone archway into the yard of a goat farm.

Thank God the Marat family wasn't around to ask me what was going on. As I fled I'd made the decision to go on the run again. Hiding was not an option on this small island. These guys were good to have found me in the first place. How had they done that? And Rob and Brad turning up the same week. How coincidental was that? Was Rob working for them, or what? But how come he ended up dead in my apartment?

I ran through the barn, opened a small door at the end, and closed it behind me. In the outbuilding just beyond I grabbed my auto cycle, an ordinary bicycle with a little motor to assist going up hills, and teetered off down the hill behind the farmhouse. The trail wound through another olive grove and once I was through that without seeing any cars, I figured I was safe.

I breathed a sigh of relief, pleased that my escape plan was working. I had my grab bag with emergency supplies on my back and I stayed off the paved roads as I cycled to the north of the island. I kept going up to the marina. With hardly any groupies around the docks I was five miles out on a forty foot motor cruiser in two hours and on the Greek mainland in three days.

The Woman on the Knoll

Twenty-seven - the present

Anji came into the apartment and wrinkled her nose. "God, it stinks in here," she said. "Did you burn the toast again, Sara?"

"I guess. It did taste funny, but I was busy on my web site."

"Is that what you were working on when I went to bed at some god awful hour last night?"

"Yes, and I've been on it all day today too."

"Like I couldn't tell? Look at this place. What a mess."

"Never mind that, come see what I've done."

She led Anji into the bedroom office and sat her down in front of the laptop."

Anji read out loud.

"The president's aide stuck his head into the communications bay.

"Any news?"

No response. He leaned in further and saw the radio operator hunched over the console, headphones tight over his ears. He tapped the airman on the shoulder and got an irritated wave from one hand as the other frantically scribbled on a message pad.

He waited, the cigarette burning down between his fingers. The muffled air stream noise from outside seemed louder as he stood there and watched the spiraling smoke get sucked into the overhead vent."

Anji looked up at Sara. "Are you nuts? Why have you put your first chapter out on the web? Who's going to buy the book if you publish it for free?"

"It's a tease. I only put twenty pages on the site. But you haven't seen the best yet. Look at this."

She leaned over Anji and brought up a new window. She read out loud, "What a load of garbage. Who in their right mind could write this crap?"

"Ohmigod. What's that?" Anji said.

"it's on the message board I set up. It's had 95 hits."

Anji looked up and saw Sara's eyes were wide open.

"It's humungous, Anji, and growing faster than I can read it. Listen to this one, You have a fertile imagination, but Kennedy is not dead, they spirited him away. And this one, Women can't shoot straight, everyone knows that, and, the CIA killed him and they hate women. That's why they'd never use one to kill JFK. It's going viral and as word spreads, especially when I link it into all the Kennedy web sites out there the publicity will be huge. I can use all the interest to sell the book."

"Cool. Let's have some wine and we can talk."

"You must be joking, I've got all this to read." Sara said.

"Come into the living room and then sit down and shut up. You're going to drink some wine and listen to me."

Anji went through to the kitchen and came back

with a bottle and three glasses.

"Why three?" Sara said.

"Because a friend's coming round who wants to meet you."

"Who?" Anji was always trying to help Sara.

"I just said. An old friend."

"No." Sara didn't always want Anji's help.

"You haven't met him yet."

"And I don't want to," Sara said. But, intrigued, she said, "Who is he?"

"I've known him a while. We were an item a year or so ago."

"Another one you used and threw back?"

"Exactly, dear Sara. Now if you'll be quiet I'll tell you why you guys should meet. I first met him at a business lunch when we were negotiating a company merger. Of all the dweebs at the table he was the only one who looked at all interesting and I made sure to sit next to him."

"And then played footsy?"

"Only a little, it was business after all. Don't interrupt. And drink some wine; it'll make you less aggressive. His name's Nicholas van der Meer and he's gorgeous. Pretty good in the sack too but that's beside the point."

Sara almost shouted. "So what is the point, Anji?"

"The point, my darling, is that he's an agent."

Sara stared at her. "What kind of agent?" Ice could have formed around the words. "FBI, CIA, Special, Secret, Travel…?"

Anji ignored Sara and continued. "A literary agent. I showed him those chapters you let me read and he wants to talk to you about the novel."

"Tell him to get lost. I'm not interested. I choose my own agent, editor, and publisher, so don't foist some ex-boyfriend jerk on me."

"Don't be so hasty, Sara. You told me you needed a new agent and he's..."

The intercom buzzed and a European accent announced "Anji, it's Nicholas van der Meer."

Sara glared and said, "Don't let him up," but Anji pressed the entry button.

"You let him in and I walk," Sara said. "Even if he's the best agent in New York."

"Oh come on, Sara. Nicky's great."

The doorbell rang and Sara said, "Don't you dare..."

Anji stared at Sara, laughed, and said, "Double dare," then opened the door. A tall figure in a long black coat came in, trailing a splatter of water off the hem.

"Disgusting." He said. "Filthy night." He sniffed. "And what's that smell? Is something burning?"

Sara went into her bedroom office and grabbed her coat. As she started for the doorway the tall, but now coat less black suited figure was looking at her.

"Sara. I've been longing to meet you ever since Anji mentioned you. You have a great imagination and we could make a monster bestseller out of this."

Sara stared up at him. "We? You arrogant..."

Anji said, "Sara, give him a chance, he's a great agent. He represented Jack Ashworth with his Cold War series - got a great deal on the movie rights too."

Sara approached.

He held out his hand. "Nicholas van der Meer, but

The Woman on the Knoll

please call me Nicky."

Sara shook her head. "I know you guys are trying to help but I really don't want it. Thanks but no thanks."

"But Sara, you said yourself that you needed a new agent after Tom Beresford retired."

"And I'll find my own, thanks very much. Who knows, I might even self-publish and print-on-demand. And there's always Kindle and other ebooks out there. Why would I want this guy?"

"Think of it as a vote of confidence."

"In me?"

"Yes."

Sara shook her head. "I don't understand."

"You know J. K. Rowling."

Sara nodded. "Oh yeah. We had lunch yesterday!"

"Sara!"

"Okay Anji. What are you talking about?"

Nicholas interrupted and said, "Harry Potter was turned into a multi-billion dollar industry. I can do the same for you."

Sara turned to face him. "You're just an agent. How can you be so su re you can find me a publisher?"

"That's the beauty of it, Sara," Anji said, interrupting. "I told you I met Nicky at a meeting about a merger? It was combining Nicky's agent business into Meer's publishing. What d'you think about that?"

"Anji, he only did that to diddle authors out of more money. He'll get his 10 or 15% as agent plus the profit from publishing the hard copy. I'll bet a third company is an e-book business, right?"

"Well, yes, but…"

"No buts, Anji."

Nicholas van der Meer stepped forward again to shake her hand. Sara saw a hesitant smile on his face.

"No," she said.

Nicholas frowned and opened his mouth to speak.

"Don't," Sara said and broke into a smile. She stepped past him and swung her coat around her shoulders. He moved to the side but didn't notice the coffee table that bumped the back of his leg. He fell backwards heavily. Sara stepped over his crumpling body and left the apartment.

Twenty-eight

Where does a woman go on a wet and windy night where she won't get hassled? And wants to check out some facts? The library. It's usually quiet and you can Google from there as easily as from home. Sara found a public terminal and logged into her email account. Conspiracy theorists were having a field day with her ideas and her in-box was full. Filtering the nuggets out of the dross was demanding but she was ruthless. Any hint of flakiness or a whack job and she deleted the entry. The penis enhancements, financial adverts, African fraud schemes and cheap medication sites were easy to find and delete, as were the messages signed JFK or RFK. Emails from Che Guevara and Fidel Castro claimed to have killed both Kennedy brothers but then so did the ones from the mobsters Sam Giancana and Traficante Jnr., mobsters, both of whom were dead, but who had been suspected as conspirators. Obviously she was attracting all kinds of Kennedy nuts.

Sara had a harder time with some of the more intelligent entries. They were harder to figure out. She stared at the screen and read the seventeen emails that were left. She kept three from literary agents, two from publishers, and four from multimedia companies inquiring about licensing for games and/or movie rights discussions in a new folder labeled Biz. That left eight. She smiled. Getting some order in the emails was a small triumph. Then she paused, thinking about poor Nicholas. He'd arrived in good faith at Anji's request, not anticipating an antagonistic reception and she now realized that her anger should have been directed at Anji for not consulting her in advance. She thought of excuses. Stress? Being pissed off about her current lack of control over her life? Wondering where the hell her novel was going? And truth be told, she did need a new agent. She shook her head, knowing that she had to get back to Nicholas and apologize. But not quite yet. She recognized that she was stalling but rationalized that checking the rest of the emails had a higher priority.

The first was succinct.

Hi Sara. I'm fascinated by your new angle on a subject which has been analyzed to death over the years. This idea is controversial, and intriguing. I would love to discuss it further with you KT

Content free but he sounds earnest, Sara thought. The next two explained in excruciating detail what they thought of a woman sniper. Another had some interesting observations about the process of breaking down the rifle into concealable pieces, but others suggested NRA to her.

A further three claimed to be from the FBI, the Secret Service, and some other unnamed agency. They had a sense of official bureaucracy that Sara thought lifted them above the crassness of the false emails that she had discarded. The next email was on behalf of the Kennedy Assassination Market which listed a bunch of 'miserabelia'.

The Woman on the Knoll

You want a piece of Dealey Plaza sod? A replica rifle? A bloodstained pink suited Jackie doll? Ambulance chasers had nothing on these ghouls. She trashed the email.

The final email on the keeper list was another from KT.

'This may sound kooky, but I figure that if it's enough to worry me, then I should let you know about it too. Last night my office was broken into. The burglars did not want money or valuables, just took my computer and paper files. I was lucky. I keep all my Kennedy files in secure storage. Nothing else I work on is as sensitive so I have to assume that is what they were looking for. I suggest that you take care.'

Holy shit. Sara looked round the library. She wondered why she had assumed KT was male and the decided that printing his two emails on a shared printer wasn't a good idea. Apart from the chance of someone else picking them up before she did, she was worried that a server somewhere would keep a record of files printed. The intrusive Patriot Act meant that nothing was safe from the government's prying eyes, even if libraries did delete personal records as soon as possible. She realized her paranoia was being nurtured by KT but she felt his anguish coming through the emails, and her gut told her he was sincere.

She emailed him and got an instant reply.
Are you on your own computer?
No.
Good. Keep it that way. They'll be slower tracing you.
Who?
FBI, Secret Service, CIA...

Why? And what Kennedy records and why do you keep a bunch of them?

I'm not going to trust that info over the net. Let's meet in person.

She thought quickly.

Okay...there's a bistro on 63rd Street near 10th Avenue. Meet me there in an hour. Carry a cell phone in your left hand.

Twenty-nine

Twenty minutes later she was sitting at a bar window seat looking across a road at the bistro. She counted eight customers going in and six coming out, none carrying a cell phone.

After an hour, having rebuffed three patrons with dubious but unambiguous intent, she left.

"Dammit."

She never swore, but today.... So now what? Back to Anji's and apologize? Sara sighed, and kept a fast pace along 69th. She was feeling increasingly guilty about Nicky, even though Anji shouldn't have invited him without asking her first. They had both wanted to help, so maybe she should reconsider. She thought about Nicky. She did need a new agent, but Anji only brought him along as a favor between two old friends. He had represented Jack Ashworth who was a respectable author so he must be pretty good, but what about fiction? Had he negotiated any good deals with novels? Only one way to check him out.

She hailed a cab.

Thirty

Tom Melville had represented Sara for all of her published books. She'd had another agent early on but he'd failed her miserably. In three years he'd sold nothing for her. Later she'd discovered that he took on almost every author who applied to him and once he'd tried a couple of times to place a book with a publisher, he'd give up and move on to another author's books. A wiser older author that she met at the San Francisco Writers Conference had sympathized with her and read one of her books. Tom was her agent and she recommended Sara to him. He'd taken her on and made her a living wage for five years until a heart attack forced him into retirement. Then he gave Sara three names of agencies that he thought could represent her well, but she hadn't made any decision yet. She wanted to finish The Woman on the Knoll before looking for the best agent to represent her new baby.

Sara stood outside the old brownstone as the cab pulled away. She saw the lights were on in Tom's first floor apartment and buzzed the doorbell.

No response.

Even leaning on the buzzer continuously didn't work.

She pressed all the apartment buttons until someone on the fourth floor finally answered.

"Waddya want?" came a male voice, deep and gruff.

"I'm here to see Tom Melville."

"Who?"

"Tom Melville. He's in the first floor apartment."

"So ring his bell..."

Before he could break the connection, Sara interrupted. "Wait a minute. He's not answering but his lights are on."

"Sounds like a bad joke, lady. Is he the guy in number three? The crotchety old man?"

Sara laughed. "That sounds right."

She heard a long sigh. "He's a miserable old bugger."

Sara waited for him to say more, but the intercom burped and died. "Shit!"

She started to hit the remaining buttons, but then the door clicked. He must have believed her. Sara pushed the door and it opened. She went into the brightly lit lobby and saw the mailboxes lining one wall. Number three was open, and empty. She walked through, turned right, and right again until she came to Tom's door. It was closed. She pressed his bell button and waited. Nothing. She knocked loudly and called, "Tom. Open the door." Nothing, not a sound.

She tentatively tried the door handle. It moved under her gentle pressure and she opened it slowly. She peered through the small crack but saw nothing unusual, then drew a deep breath and pushed the door so that it swung fully open. The small entryway and living room beyond looked normal. Tom's piles of books littered every horizontal surface and overflowed onto the floor. Sara stepped in and pulled the door closed behind her.

"Tom...? Tom?"

Nothing.

She walked through the living room. Tom's bedroom and bathroom were to the left, and his study/den to the right. She could see that the bed was undisturbed but wondered why the only room with no light on was the study. She went to its doorway and flicked the light switch up.

She drew in a sharp breath. Tom was lying on the floor with blood oozing from a small head wound. Sara knelt over him. He was unconscious and lying on his side. She put her face down near his and could feel his breath and see his chest slowly rising and falling. She checked his head wound and was relieved to see only a small cut and that the blood was already clotting. He didn't seem to need any immediate first aid, so she left him as he was and went to his phone on the desk.

"Ambulance...""

"53 Ormerod Place...apartment number three...no...no...Thomas Melville...he's been assaulted in his home...yes, this address...I don't know..."

Sara put the phone down and figured she had a minimum of three minutes before the emergency services could arrive. She saw that two out of three of Tom's filing cabinets were open and papers were strewn over the floor. Why? Who would want information from a retired literary agent? She quickly scanned the mess but saw no reason for the chaos. She leaned back against the desk. The only logical answer as to why one filing cabinet was not open

The Woman on the Knoll

was that the intruder had found the information he wanted. Sara assumed it had been a 'he' for no other reason than the attack on an old man, and the mess in the room. A woman was less likely to have hurt Tom and would not have trashed the place.

She looked around again. The phone! She wiped the plastic receiver with a Kleenex and also the keys 9 and 1. Two sheets of paper on the desk caught her eye. She flipped them round to read them and saw her name at the top. Why would...? Then she saw her cellphone number and Anji's address written prominently on the second sheet.

"Shit!" Too many thoughts flashed through her mind but they all coalesced into one.

"Anji!"

She fled from the apartment, knocking into a young guy who was just entering the lobby.

"Hey!"

She heard his rasping voice of complaint as she rushed out the entry door and down the steps.

Thirty-one

Sara walked a couple of blocks then slowed and called Anji. No answer. She tried again. Nothing. Then she called a cab. She was pacing the sidewalk when a taxi finally arrived.

"16 Excelsior, and hurry please."

The cabbie nodded and put his foot down.

She tried calling Anji again; still no response.

As the taxi made the final turn toward the apartment block and Sara was reaching for her purse, she saw heard sirens and then saw flashing lights. The road ahead was full of cop cars, three fire trucks, and two ambulances. The paramedics were working on one person lying on the sidewalk and the firefighters were pulsing huge jets of water up to the third and fourth floors.

"Don't believe it…I just don't believe it," she muttered.

"You live up there, Miss?"

"Stop here," Sara said, handing the driver a fistful of small bills.

She looked up at the apartment block and heard the taxi turn in the narrow street. Flames raged out of the third floor windows and black oily smoke drifted past her.

The cops had rigged yellow warning tape to keep spectators back. How could a flimsy piece of plastic do that? A part of her mind wondered how that worked while the larger piece screamed out, 'what the hell happened here?'

She maneuvered through the crowd toward a cop and said, "I've got a friend lives in there, number 33 on the third floor Do you know if..."

"Dunno lady, and I couldn't tell you if you was Katie Couric down here asking...now get outa here and let us do our job."

Sara pouted her lips and forced out some tears, which in truth had not been far away. "But my friend Anji lives up there," she sobbed, clutching the cop's arm. His attention had been caught by a gold trimmed uniform as it waved him forward and as he shrugged her off he shouted,"GET outa here!" His words could be plainly heard over the noise farther down the street as a wall disintegrated near the top of the building.

Sara sobbed for real now, picturing her friend up there. She turned away from the blazing building.

"Sara!"

She couldn't see who shouted nor did she recognize the voice, but she did see a head turn from a different direction and look at her. She didn't recognize him either, but he started to lunge through people toward her. His urgency scared her and she ran. A hole opened in the crowd ahead of her and she fled up the street. She looked back as she turned the corner and saw there were now two men chasing her! WHAT?

Her previous taxi was parked up ahead.

"Thank God..." She jumped into the taxi and said,

"Get going!"

The driver looked over his shoulder and said, "Where to?"

"Dammit…" she took a breath, forcing her brain to process. "The nearest hospital." She didn't pause to wonder where that inspiration had come from and turned her head to look back at the corner. The two guys were chasing toward the taxi.

"Quickly," she shouted.

The driver roared away from the curb, his eyes on the rear view mirror.

Sara watched out of the rear window as one guy, sporting a full beard, got close enough to grab onto the taxi. The guy behind tackled him and they fell to the road in a tangle of legs and road rash.

Ten blocks later the taxi drew up in front of the ER sign.

"There you go, lady." He ran round to open the door for her as she fumbled with the handle. She rummaged in her purse for the billfold she knew was in there somewhere. He said, "It's on the house… Go!"

She ran.

The driver took his taxi to the parking area and lit a cigarette. To hell with the ordinances. He didn't have to wait long. She came back out the door and turned in the direction they'd been driving. He watched her feet stumble and her clumsy attempt to recover before she fell. She stayed upright but he worried that next time she might not.

He drove up alongside her and stopped. She stared at him as he came round and helped her into the front passenger seat.

Thirty-two

Sara looked at the taxi driver.

"What is this?" she whispered, "Why did you wait?"

"I can tell when someone's in trouble, Ms. Turner."

He drove off slowly, mindful of the weirdos who roam hospital parking lots at night.

She jerked upright in her seat.

"How do you know my name?"

"Doesn't take much brainpower," he said, "Your photo is on the back cover of all your novels." He looked at her. "So is this part of the creative process? Are you on a dry run for your next book?"

A corner of her mouth twitched. She hesitated and then said, "Of course. And now I'd like you to take me to a cheap hotel where no questions are asked and the sheets get changed occasionally."

He laughed. "The guys in the bar will never believe this. I'm taking Sara Turner on location search."

He drove for ten minutes before he pulled up near the seedy entrance of a distressed building.

"What's your name?" said Sara.

"Bill. Bill Simons."

"Okay Bill Simons, you'll be a character in my next book."

He laughed again. "Let's get you safe inside."

He went round, opened her door, and took her arm to go up the steps.

"I can manage on my own, thanks."

He let her go and she staggered up the five treads, realizing that maybe she should have taken up Bill's offer. The lobby was in better shape than the exterior of the building had suggested. It was small but had a few comforts of home; two shabby but welcoming armchairs and a low table with a few recent magazines on it, some new paint smell, and fresh flowers on the counter. She surprised herself that she noticed these touches, and also that the clerk was wearing a clean shirt, not a polo or a T, but buttoned down.

Bill came in behind her. "This is Dominic," said Bill. "He's the night manager and co-owner. Dominic this is…"

"Ellen. Ellen Magister," Sara said, using the name of the hero in her last book.

Dominic looked at her and one eye closed briefly. He laughed and said, "Anything to accommodate you," then he dropped his voice by about forty decibels, "Sara, you're my favorite author."

Bill saw Sara's expression and he smiled. "I used to help Dominic with his grammar and I pass all my books on to him to improve his English."

Sara said, "You must be a very good friend, but won't the author object to the loss of royalties?"

Dominic looked thunderstruck. "Bill, you did not tell me of this. We must pay Ms…"

The Woman on the Knoll

"Magister," Sara said quickly. "But seeing as Ellen Magister doesn't write any books, then obviously there can't be any loss of income."

Bill laughed again, and after Dominic had worked through the faulty logic, he smiled too, grabbed a key from under the counter and slid it across to Bill.

"You'd better help Ms. Magister up to her room, Bill, she looks tired."

Sara looked at him as she swayed and clung to the edge of the counter. She nodded and felt Bill's arm round her "Geddoff..." she said, feeling dozy and grumpy. She laughed a nervous cackle. "Did you hear that?" she said. "Dozy and Grumpy?"

Dominic, mouth open and brow wrinkled, looked at Bill. His unspoken question drew a quizzical shrug. Then Bill said, "Which floor?"

"Top," said Dominic, his gaze switching back to Sara. "Is she going to be...?"

Bill cut him off in mid-sentence. "She'll be fine after a good night's sleep. Are you on all night?"

"Yeah. Why?"

"Because I don't want anyone wandering in off the street and hassling her."

"Mr. Bill, I no let that happen." Dominic sometimes lost his new found language skills in times of stress. "She pretty author who needs help."

"She sure is. You got her latest behind there?"

"Yeah." Dominic pulled a well thumbed copy from under the counter.

Bill took it, his nose twitching as he smelled hot chili. "Got your dinner there too?"

Dominic nodded and smiled.

"Can I get to my room, guys?"

Bill had almost forgotten why they were there.

"Just one minute," he said, turning the book over. A synopsis of the plot and characters occupied the top half of the back cover, with author details below. He remembered her first book had just the plot on the back cover and a brief bio tucked away inside somewhere. Now that she was an established author, her readers wanted more information about her.

Bill jabbed a finger at her picture. "There we go. Prettier in real life..."

"Goddammit, I want to go to my room!" shouted Sara.

A new customer just walking in turned and walked out.

"Bill, get her upstairs! I got girls coming and going with older men if you know what I mean..."

They got. The elevator worked, albeit asthmatically. The room was spacious, clean, and smelled of roses. Red roses, scattered across the bed.

"What the hell...?" said Sara.

The phone on the nightstand chirped.

"Bill? It's Dominic."

"Who the hell else would it be?" growled Bill, as he watched Sara throw her jeans and shirt into the corner of the room, climb into bed, curl up, and close her eyes.

"I gave you the wrong room," Dominic said. "You're supposed to be next door, in the Girls' overflow room."

"And we should we care because...?"

"Because I've got a girl here now with a rich-looking dude."

The Woman on the Knoll

"So let her overflow."

"But she's a regular, and hot too. Gets a lot of high rollers."

"Round here? Oh, the roses, right?"

"Mr. Bill, please."

"Look, Dominic. Apart from the fact that Sara Turner's already asleep on the well pounded mattress, do you remember her third book? The guys who rescued the girl? Well tonight we're the heroes."

Bill heard a sigh and knew that Ms. Twinkle thighs would be getting a smaller room for the night's Johns.

He decided to toss Dominic a bone. "Plus we're now quits for the lessons." Bill heard a distant jingle of keys just before he was cut off. One issue solved. Now for the big question. Stay here with her or come back in the morning? No option of course. He'd done his bit, she'd be okay now. He scribbled a note on the hotel writing pad and opened the door.

The fist hit him once. That was all he remembered in the morning.

Thirty-three

Ken Tierney sat on his restored 1960 Panhead DuoGlide with the white hard shell saddle bags and wondered where Sara had got to. He had tucked the bike into the curb just off 69th and 14th between a Ford and a Chevy. He could see the little Bistro and was five minutes early for their meeting. He knew what she looked like from his research on the web, and she sure as hell hadn't gone in while he was waiting. He checked up and down the quiet sidewalks. No sign of her. He could feel the cold drizzle seeping down his neck. The only warm parts of him were his legs straddling the engine which idled with its characteristic 'bloomp, bloomp'. He'd spent five years tracking down original parts for the bike; eBay was his friend and partner. He shifted his weight on the saddle to tilt the bike to the right so he could lift his left foot up out of the water streaming down the gutter.

A woman emerged from a bar across from the Bistro. He couldn't see her face as she waved for a cab but she seemed to be the right height for Sara Turner. She turned in his direction to check for traffic and he saw her features clearly. Dammit. If she'd been here all the time why hadn't she gone into the Bistro? For the same reason

The Woman on the Knoll

that I didn't, he thought. Guess we were both being careful.

He pulled out into traffic and followed her cab for five minutes. When it stopped he pulled over and killed the engine. She got out and walked up the steps to a tall brownstone and leaned on the bell until she was let in. The door closed behind her. He saw her shadow on a curtain on the first floor and then a light came on in another room. He waited.

After five minutes he saw a man turn the corner and walk toward the brownstone. He watched him go in through the door but before it had closed Sara came running out and along the sidewalk.

It was hard to follow her with the bike and he didn't want to start the engine in case she heard it. Then he couldn't push the bike fast enough to keep up with her. She disappeared around a corner maybe two hundred yards ahead and he had to make a choice. He propped the Harley on its stand and ran to the corner. He saw Sara on the sidewalk speaking on her phone. It was a short conversation and when she put down the phone she paced up and down and just seemed to be killing time. He took a chance and ran back to his bike. He started it and rode slowly back to the corner. He looked round it just in time to see Sara getting into another taxi.

He followed her cab as it sped through the grimy streets, speeding where it was safe to do so. In five minutes it screeched to a halt near a burning building.

From fifty yards away he watched as she ran up to a crowd surrounding an apartment fire and shouldered her way through. Ken never liked leaving his pride and joy alone in the city, but for once entrusted the bike to the six foot rubber protected 2000# breaking strain chain with its seven-way titanium combo lock and helmet linkage. He followed her into the crowd, feeling the heat of the fire on his forehead.

She went up to a cop who seemed to have a dismissive conversation with her and left her looking even more distressed. Ken watched as she turned away in the crowd. He didn't want to lose her so he shouted her name. She looked over her shoulder but didn't see him. Then he saw another guy look up, startled at her name, and start pushing through the crowd toward her. She headed away from him. The guy followed her and Ken went after both of them.

Sara ran round the corner. Ken was following ten feet behind the other guy's pounding white Nikes as he rounded the corner. Sara was climbing into a taxi which moved away quickly. Nike guy made a lunge for the trunk but Ken leaped on him and hauled him back. They crashed to the ground, Ken on top.

"Shit!"

Ken bent over gasping. The taxi accelerated and disappeared round a corner.

"Dammittohell!"

Ken jumped as a blast of a horn came from behind him and he realized he was in the middle of the street. He puffed his way to the sidewalk and stood there breathing hard, leaving Nike guy in the road. The driver leaned on his horn and the guy unpeeled himself from the blacktop and staggered away. Ken saw that he had a beard.

Ken was pissed. He'd been so close to catching her. He ran back round the corner, unlocked the chain and fired up his Harley. Thirty seconds later he was roaring up the road after the taxi. Three blocks later he caught up and

The Woman on the Knoll

followed it to the hospital, and then to the hotel. He gave Sara a few minutes to get settled and then went into the lobby. The night person was giving a leggy blonde woman and an older guy a room key. She was bitching big time about wanting her usual room #37.

"Dominic, you'd better give not give my room away again or I'll go elsewhere."

Ken smiled and asked for a room. He got #21. He used the stairs rather than the asthmatic elevator and kept going up to the third floor.

He walked to door #37 and paused, wondering how he could introduce himself to her before she screamed. His problem was solved when the door opened, and before he knew it he'd hit the taxi driver.

Thirty-four

Ken stared as the taxi driver crumpled to the floor. He'd assumed that Sara would be alone and he hadn't been able to control his instinctive 'fight or flight' response when someone else opened the door. Now he'd screwed things up. How could he talk to her with a body sprawled across the bedroom floor?

He looked around. He didn't think the bathroom would work to hide the body because that's the first place you go when you when you wake up. The closet? Too small. 'Hide in plain view,' the instructor, what was his name, oh yes, 'Brad, but call me Sir', used to say. What about in the bath with the shower curtain pulled? She might not see him there.

He pulled the unconscious form toward the bathroom, his chest soon heaving under the weight of the sedentary taxi driver. "Come on..." he whispered to himself, "this should be easy after all that training. Yeah sure," he answered himself, "but that was twenty years ago."

He dragged the taxi driver's body up over the rim and into the tub then made sure he was breathing okay. Now that he had the guy almost concealed he checked for a wallet. Turned out the guy he'd assaulted was a William Smith. He shrugged. "Sorry Bill," he whispered, then closed the shower curtain, and checked the shadowy figure inside the tub. Maybe he should bend Bill's legs so he could slide his head and shoulders down into the tub more. He tried but then Bill's knees stuck up too far.

"The hell with it." He sank down on the cork tile floor, his back against the tub. "Oh, shit." He lowered his head to think through the consequences of the last ten minutes. Ever since the door opened in his face he'd been acting on instinct, fear, and adrenaline, and although close to panic, he'd kept his head clear. He replayed the events since he'd stood in the hallway outside the door. What else could have done? Well, not hitting the guy would have been a good start.

A loud groan from the tub scared the crap out of him and he looked round to check on Bill.

Thirty-five

Sara jerked awake. A noise had woken her and it hadn't been a normal building creak. She held her breath. The room light was still on and nothing looked out of place. Then she heard a rustling noise from the bathroom. Mice? Rats? No, this wasn't rodent paws scrabbling, it was more deliberate. Was Bill Simpson still here?

Then the noise stopped.

Ten seconds passed.

Her chest hurt and her oxygen starved lungs shouted at her. She opened her mouth wide to exhale and then breathed in. She slid out of bed on the side away from the bathroom door. As she stood on the floor she heard a deep breath of exertion followed by mumbling sounds. There was a definite someone rather than a something in the bathroom. Louder muttering was followed by a hollow thump. Later a voice said "Sorry, Bill."

Sara froze. So Bill was in there, but someone else was with him? Who? What was going on? She shivered, and quietly pulled on her shirt, jeans and shoes. She moved toward the bathroom door, grabbing her purse from the table on the way. As she passed the bathroom door she saw the back of a man in there, facing away as he talked round the shower curtain into the bathtub.

"Okay, Bill, you just have a quiet nap in there..."

Somehow a stranger had overcome Bill and had hidden him in the tub. Sara couldn't hear any water running so she didn't think Bill was in immediate danger. She saw the intruder had short curly brown hair and wore a crumpled leather jacket. He looked like one of the guys who had chased her taxi. She crossed the room, opened the door and ran to the stairs. Stumbling over the treads she half fell down the second flight but arrived in the lobby without too much damage.

Dominic jumped up from his stool behind the counter, his paperback flying over the counter. His mouth opened, but Sara beat him to it. "Dominic, call 911! There's a burglar in my room and he's hurt Bill. Hurry!"

Dominic was slow to catch on but once Sara saw the meaning of the words register she fled from the lobby. She ran along the street until she reached a recognizable world of Starbucks and shopping malls. After another two blocks she reached an area where running along the sidewalk without ear buds might seem suspicious so she slowed to a walk and then ducked into a 24 hour supermarket. In the restroom she sank onto the toilet seat and shivered. As her pulse rate slowed she looked at the cracked and dirty tiles, the stains on the floor and walls, and the crooked towel dispenser hanging to the side of the sink. Another shiver, this time from distaste. Had to be a guy who looked after this mess. She checked her distorted reflection in the buckled metal mirror above the greasy sink. Jeez, she told herself. You look like you should be back in the flophouse. Not feeling comfortable with washing anything but her hands in this bathroom, she lathered. At least the soap comes out of a dispenser, she muttered, and rinsed without touching the sink. She rubbed her hands on her jeans and used a sheet of TP, from down in the roll, to open the door.

There was a kid waiting outside, hopping from one foot to the other. His Mom was tapping her fingers against her purse. "It's hardly worth the wait," Sara said, then wondered why she had him shopping with her at this time of night.

"Wait till you've got kids," the woman replied and darted in, dragging the little boy behind her. Sara heard the kid say, "Phooey," as she walked away through the produce section.

Sara needed shelter and security but she was running out of options. She went to the coffee shop in the corner of the store, bought an Americano and a stale cheesecake, and sat at a table partly concealed behind a plastic ficus tree. She was tired. Tears ran down her cheeks as she replayed the day. She had one last place she could stay and one phone call would arrange it. She felt inside her purse, but her hand started that twitchy, 'Oh on, I can't believe it's not here!' panic. She looked inside the purse, then laid it on the table, and started pulling the contents out.

"Aw, crap."

The guy at the next table looked over in surprise. One stare back from her dirty face and disheveled hair soon put him in his place. She looked at the strewn contents of her purse. Where was her cell phone? She couldn't remember when she'd last had it.

The guy next door was examining his newspaper with great attention. She didn't want to spook him or give him anything else to remember her by so she repacked her purse, swigged some coffee, finished her cheesecake, and went to the counter to get some quarters. "And is there a payphone near here?"

Two blocks along, in a trashed booth outside a 7-11 where she felt reasonably safe, she was surprised to get a dial tone. She dialed a number from memory. The person at the other end took a long time to answer.

"Hi, it's me," she said, before the other person could say a word.

"Sara? Is there a problem?" came the voice.

"Listen, I don't have much time…you have to get out of there."

"Sara, tell me what's going on."

"Just do it! I'll see you at Jake's...Go!"

Sara hoped she'd stuck with the 30 second limit they'd agreed on at the beginning and put the phone down. She turned to leave the booth and walked straight into a guy standing there. She bounced back off his chest. His suit jacket was unbuttoned and she noticed its red silk lining. His tie was fashionably slim and a contrasting blue. She looked up into his eyes and saw a reassuring smile spread across his face. He grabbed her right arm to steady her and said, "Hello Sara."

Thirty-six

Ken was re-arranging Bill's knees and didn't hear Sara's soft footsteps across the carpet, but he did hear the click of the lock as the door closed. He left Bill in the tub and groaned as he eased himself up from his knees. In the bedroom he saw the rumpled bedclothes and the cell phone on the floor. He grabbed it and ran to the door.

He couldn't hear the elevator moving or the sound of her feet on the stairs. He went to the far end of the hall and crashed down the bare concrete steps of the emergency stairs and out through the steel exit door. He ran to his bike. His chances of catching her were slight, but if she were still on the street fronting the hotel he had a chance. He roared up the alley behind the hotel. Midway along the block he saw too late, and couldn't avoid, a pallet. He went over the handlebars and landed with a huge impact on some cardboard boxes which had overflowed from a dumpster. He staggered up winded, but without the broken bones he might have suffered from crashing directly into the dumpster.

He gathered his wits and his breath, and checked his bike. The front wheel was buckled. Tires he could get easily, but an original wheel? He'd taken six months to find

The Woman on the Knoll

this one. He limped round to the main street. He stood on the corner rubbing his knee as he checked both ways along the street. There was no way to tell which direction she'd gone, so he turned left and started walking. His knee hurt more as he put weight on it and his pace was reduced to a hobbling limp.

An hour later he was in agony and turned into an all night store to buy some Tylenol. He found a mega-jumbo pack and waited in line behind a street person who was hassling the counter clerk.

"I tell you the hotdog was stale, man."

"Then why did you eat it all before you came back and complained."

"Cos I was too hungry, but now I feel sick. You owe me another."

"Why? First off it wasn't stale, I put those in fresh when I came on shift at ten. Second, if it made you sick then you won't be able to eat another, will you? Now get out of here."

Ken leaned on the counter, taking the weight off his bad leg.

"When you guys are done, I'm in pain here." He smacked the pill bottle down on the counter and pushed a twenty towards the clerk. "Finish your fight later, will ya?"

The two of them looked at him.

The street person said, "We're not fighting. I come in here every night to get warm and while I'm a customer he can't throw me out. Plus he likes the company, don't you, Mohammed."

"My name is Singh, not Mohammed. Can't you tell the difference between a Muslim turban and this?" He pointed to his head. "I am a Sikh. I keep telling you this, why can't you remember that, huh?"

"Hey, I just want to pay for my pills," Ken said, as his attention was grabbed by movement outside the store. "Dammit," he whispered. Through the illuminated Bud sign hanging in front of the window he thought he saw Sara. Why would she be outside? He hobbled to one side and saw that she was standing by a payphone talking to a man in a suit. He moved toward the door.

"What about your change?" said the clerk. "And your pills?"

Ken ignored him and stepped outside, wincing with the effort. He called her name, "Sara...?"

Thirty-seven

"Who are you?" Sara said, still looking into the red lining stranger's eyes.

"How about someone who can help you?"

Sara shrugged her arm away from his grip and leaned away from him. She felt the Plexiglas of the payphone booth dig into her shoulder. "What does that mean?"

His jacket flapped in the breeze, flashing red again.

"Well?" she said.

"Would you stop shouting if I told you?"

"I'm not shouting!" She paused and realized she was. "Oh."

He waited until her face relaxed. "I'm with the FIA." He flashed a badge, waving it briefly in front of her.

"What the hell is the FIA?"

"The Federal Intelligence Agency. We work with Homeland Security."

She shook her head. "Never heard of it. And doesn't the FBI do that?"

He smiled and said, "They help, yes. But we report to the director of Homeland Security and not the Justice Department."

He was six inches taller than her, expensively dressed and hair beautifully cut. He had a dark complexion with a Mediterranean look, and in a crowded bar she'd have checked him out more than once. But that was no reason to trust him. And why did he want to help her?

"How do you know my name?"

"We've been keeping an eye on you ever since you put your website out there. You've attracted a lot of attention and now it's getting too dangerous for you to be out on your own."

She looked at him, his confident manner calming her. "And...?" Then his words sank in. "What do you mean, dangerous?"

"The people who have been chasing you are getting too close; We need to protect you now."

"What people?"

"The ones that don't like the sort of memories that you're stirring up."

Sara checked him over again. Elegant shoes and clothes, smooth manner, but a heavy stubble on his chin.

"Why should I trust you? All I've seen is a cheap ID card that you could have made at Kinko's."

He looked at her. "We both want answers, Sara. There are a couple of government agencies who'd love to talk to you. We've got a safe house nearby. You want to come?"

He seemed sincere, but then so had most everyone else she'd met recently. He leaned on his car and waited. Sara sighed as she pondered her options. The old Martha and the Vandellas song that her grandmother used to play, nowhere to go, nowhere to hide, flashed through her mind. Then she saw a disheveled figure limp out of the 7-11. She

The Woman on the Knoll

recognized him from outside Anji's apartment and remembered he was one of the two men chasing her taxi.

She looked back at him. "What's your name?"

"Scott," he said. "Now, do you want my help or not?"

"Sara..." The guy from the 7-11 was calling her name. How did he know who she was?

"Okay, let's go," she said to Scott.

She got in the car.

"You okay?" he asked when they hit the first stop light.

"I think so."

"Who was that guy back at the store?"

"I don't know, but he'd been following me tonight. Where are you taking me? And why have you been looking for me? And why are you helping me?"

"That's a lot of questions," he said. "I told you, we're going to a safe house that the FIA has nearby. You'll be able to catch up on your missing sleep, recover some sanity, and then help us."

"How can I help you guys?"

"We're running our own investigation into the Kennedy assassinations."

"What?"

"I'll tell you more later on, for now why don't...?"

She looked at him, her suspicions running wild. "Why would Homeland Security be interested in a 50 year old killing?"

"I can't tell you that. My boss will decide if you have a need to know. But we're interested in you, your book, and your sources."

She started to say, "How am I supposed to ...okay

I'll go along with you for now."

She leaned back in the seat. Relief flooded her and within minutes she fell asleep.

Scott smiled.

Sara missed the rest of the drive which relieved Scott from having to deal with more awkward questions and having to make up some tedious story for having to blindfold her. He could have made it believable but he was tired too.

The Woman on the Knoll

Thirty-eight

Sara woke as the car wheels crunched over gravel. Scott drew the car to a halt in a pool of light from the porch of a faux Victorian mansion.

"Hey sleepyhead, we're here."

She looked at him through half closed eyelids. "And you're sure it's safe?"

"On my honor," he said.

Sara was so tired she ignored his Boy Scout cliché. Scott helped her up the steps and into the house.

She slept for ten hours.

They had breakfast in the bright, east facing dining room. Sara couldn't tell how old the house was but the tall ceilings and well proportioned rooms spoke of old money and bygone times. Either the FIA had a great budget or it had a good selection of confiscated properties to choose from.

The eggs were tired and the bacon half cold but she ate well, aware of Scott leaning back in his chair watching her. She finished and stared at him.

"What now?"

He smiled. "We talk," he said.

She shook her head, feeling the sticky in her hair.

Where could she get some decent shampoo and conditioner?

"No."

Scott sat up, his face hardening. The friendly rescuer suddenly seemed menacing. "What do you mean?" he said.

"Don't get me wrong, I'm grateful for what you've done, but I don't know you. I'm willing to talk if you're open with me so I need some information first. What is the FIA, who is it, where are we, who else is here, unless you cooked breakfast, and then we'll get to what you want to talk about. That's my deal."

"You don't seem to understand," he said. "I saved you yesterday, brought you to a safe location to rest up, and hoped we could discuss our mutual interests."

Sara sat forward in her seat, staring across the table at him. "I believe I already said thanks for your help and for breakfast, so why do I feel that you now need me more than I need you."

Scott nodded, his dark curls rustling across his shirt collar. "Fair enough. You won't have heard of the FIA because it's not in any list of government agencies. We deal with security issues that concern the President."

"But yesterday you said it reported to Homeland Security."

"Same thing. We're well funded, but officially we don't exist. I can't tell you more than that. You asked where we are. This house is on a hundred acre estate in New Hampshire, but you won't be told the address. As to the people here, we have seven total, including the necessary security to safeguard our business."

Sara sneered, letting her doubt show through her

body language. "That's a load of crap, Scott. You've told me nothing."

"You're right, and that's our security. As I said, we don't exist, but the only reason I've said as much as I have, is that we think we can trust you. And because you have an edge that can help us."

Sara thought about what she could bring to this weird organization. She frowned. "I'm just a writer. What is it that I've got?" She thought she already knew the answer but she felt it was important that Scott verbalize it.

"You're a novelist who is causing huge waves on the web with the first chapters of your book.. You've re-publicized an historic event. Even those not born when JFK died are intrigued by the shooting and all the conspiracy theories. After Oliver Stone's movie Congress started a new investigation, but that only meandered around. Maybe your theory can shed more light on the assassination."

Scott's face was flushed as he rushed his words out.

Sara could see his sincerity but… "Okay Scott, I've developed some ideas that seem to resonate with people. But it's just fiction, a novel. Something I've made up using a female assassin. What's so special about that?"

Scott squirmed on his bentwood chair at the table. "Let's move to the easy chairs by the fire," he said. "Take your cup and I'll bring the coffee pot over."

They moved into the chairs flanking the hearth. An uneasy fire smoked until Scott arranged some new logs on it. He pointed to second pile of wood and said, "Hardwood is better for heat and longer burning, but this pine is better for kick-starting a lazy fire."

Sara stirred her coffee as he rambled on.

Scott saw her fingers drumming on the side table.

"So here's the deal," he said.

"No. Wait a minute. Earlier you mentioned a conspiracy. Are you sure?"

Scott smiled. "Sixty percent of Americans believe so."

"So do the weirdos and kooks emailing me about the novel. Okay it's a topic of interest, but he was killed in 1963. That's almost 50 years ago."

"And five years later Bobby followed him. As far as we're concerned both of these killings are still open. We need to solve them while the people involved are still alive and we're running out of time to see justice done. Why won't you help us?"

"I didn't say I wouldn't, Scott, but I just can't see how my book can help. I made it up, it's…"

"It's believable fiction," Scott said, interrupting her.

"Okay," she said, looking Scott in the eye, "Tell me what you want."

Scott smiled. Sara wondered why she'd thought him good-looking when she first saw him. Because he'd helped her she guessed, but now there was like an aura around him. She'd never thought of herself as fey or subject to whim or weird spirits, but she now saw him in a new light that made her feel defensive.

"Just tell me your story about how the book came to life, how you created the characters and came up with the theme."

She thought about it. "Okay. I like plotting," she said. "I usually take a concept and turn it inside out. I do a 'whatif' for a character in a certain situation. That way I can test myself by trying to find ways out of the dilemmas I pose for my characters." Sara tossed her hair and raised her eyebrows at Scott. "Is that the kind of thing you want?"

"Kind of," he said, "but your characters and situations, where do they come from?"

"Easy," she said. "They're from people I meet in the street; see on TV, family members, business contacts, my own dreams and nightmares. They're extrapolations of idle thoughts, maybe triggered by events, memories, world history, or weird people."

Scott sat, chin down. Sara thought he was almost asleep, but he said, "Those are generalities. I'd like to know how this particular plot, with a woman assassin, came to you."

"Why?"

"It pertains to an ongoing investigation."

Sara pursed her lips, and cocked her head as she answered, "Yeah right. Okay, I'll humor you one more time. These things just happen. You're falling asleep one night and a thought grabs you. If you're lucky then you fret and pick at it till it gains some useful form. Some authors keep a notebook by the side of their bed. I don't, because I reckon if it's a good idea then I'll remember it when I wake up."

'Sara, I don't think you're trying very hard to help me here."

"Why would you say that? What's going on?"

Scott didn't answer.

"I need some fresh air," Sara said. She pointed to the French doors leading out to a flagstone patio. "Let's go for a walk."

Scott shook his head. "I have stuff to do," he said. "But you go and explore out there. Just be careful, the perimeter wire is alarmed and we have sensors all over the place. For our own security."

She nodded. "Of course."

Sara felt Scott's eyes on her as she crossed the room and fumbled with the french door catch. Cool air swooped in as she pushed open one of the doors. She walked across the lawn and wondered if the American people who believed in a JFK conspiracy still cared. After all the lies of Vietnam, Nixon, the cold war, Gulf 1 & 2, WMDs, did anyone care anymore? Probably just the conspiracy nuts. And her own book? As Tom, her old agent, had told her before he retired, 'You've written a few mysteries that have gotten you some name recognition, now you need a breakthrough novel. Write about something big, something people relate to. A big religious mystery like 'The Da Vinci Code', a huge family dynasty, or a rambling 1,000 year story of some country or historical place. Stonehenge has been done, and Hawaii, but what about Plymouth…you could even combine the two, one in England, the other here, through the eyes of one family? What do you think?'

She laughed at the memory.

The grounds were landscaped, barely. Grass and trees, all laid out to be easy to manage and to offer defensible lines of fire. Where did that thought come from? She'd been here less than a day and was already thinking of it as a sanctuary, although Scott's questioning was a bit weird. She walked on, thinking about his questions. What did he want?

She stopped when she bumped into the perimeter wire. She touched the inside wire. It was barbed, as was the outside one. Six strands on eight feet posts with a middle set of wires suspended on insulators. She looked at the array, wondering why the inside defenses were as strong as the ones on the outside. You'd only need that if you were as scared of people getting out as much as them getting in. She'd never been in a safe house but she assumed that agencies like the CIA could be that paranoid. She could hear traffic in the distance, roaring both ways along a busy road. No other clues as to where they were.

"Sara! Sara!" She heard her name. The calling was loud and earnest. She moved away from the fence and turned to see Scott with two heavies.

Scott shook his head. "Sara, I told you about the fence. What were you thinking?"

She looked at him, hands on hips. "So why does the fence face both ways? Are some of your guests here prisoners? Am I?"

Scott waved the two heavies away. They lumbered off toward the house.

"Sara..."

"Shut up."

"No, you be quiet. I want to help you. I have already, but you can help us too..."

"Scott. I've had it with you."

He walked closer to her and tried the comforting arm routine. She flung it off and stomped back up the trail to the house.

Scott followed, saying nothing.

Sara went in through the French doors and headed for the stairs.

Scott came through the door behind her and called, "What are you doing?"

Sara felt her heart pounding and the muscles in her face and cheeks tensing.

"Are you going to keep your part of the deal,

Sara?"

She turned and said. "I didn't make any deal. You did. They were your conditions, not mine."

"And you've still got a chance do this the easy way. What do you know?" He didn't wait for an answer. "You think you're so tough, you'll tell us before you leave."

She snorted.

Scott came closer and got in her face. "What do you know about the JFK assassination, Sara? Where did you get all the detail for your book? What else do you know? Why did you choose now to start publicizing it?"

She looked sideways at him and said, "How do you know there is more?

"Where did you get it?" he said to her, then hit her hard, a backhand to the cheek. The force of it rocked her back.

Sara was really pissed now. Her expression hardened. "What's going on? Why are you worried about my novel and website? Why would the publicity be a problem now?" Then she knew. Another 'Oh My God' moment. Her voice dropped in pitch. "You guys did it!"

She saw a flicker of confirmation in his face. "But there's more, isn't there? Why would history matter now, unless...Oh shit. No wonder you're shit scared of my book."

Scott grabbed her arm.

"Wait, Scott," said an authoritative voice.

An older man entered the room. He was tall with a full beard, blue eyes and a shaven head. He wore an elegant robe over regular trousers and shirt.

"What were you saying, my dear?"

"Who are you?" Sara said, spitting the words out.

The Woman on the Knoll

Scott grabbed her arm. "Be respectful, Sara. This is the Don."

Sara laughed. "You've been watching too many movies and TV series," she said. "The mafia are a... OW!"

Scott had tightened his grip on her arm and bent it up behind her back.

"Be gentle, Scott," said the Don, "Sara is our guest."

The pressure on Sara's arm lessened and she stamped on Scott's foot and tried to elbow him. Unfortunately he was ready for her and avoided the blow.

"Some guest, Boss," he said.

"Sit her down, Scott, and we'll have a little talk."

"Yeah, right," Sara said as she was pushed down into one of the easy chairs. She sank in the deep cushions and realized how hard it would be to get up quickly.

"So what were you about to say, Ms. Turner?"

"Was it just JFK? What about Bobby?"

"Why would you imagine we'd have wanted to harm the president or his brother?" the Don said.

She looked at him. His benevolent seeming face smiled at her and she wondered about the schemes being plotted in his brain.

"Why else would my novel matter to you?"

"You're quite correct. Your trashy little novel doesn't matter, but the ideas behind it are of some interest to us, my dear."

"Go stuff yourself."

"Such language from as erudite an author as yourself."

Sara knew he was baiting her and kept quiet.

"Where did you get your ideas, Sara? Who told

you? Who gave you the inspiration?"

"No one. I created it all in my mind."

"I don't think so," said the Don. "Do you believe her, Scott?"

"No, Boss."

"So what do you think we should do, Scott?"

"We could give her some encouragement…"

"I suppose so. What do you think, my dear?"

"If you are the pathetic remnants of the old mafia and you're this worried about my novel then you probably have know more than I do. A lot of people think you assassinated President Kennedy because Bobby was the Attorney General and gunning for the mob. You cut the ground from under Bobby by killing his brother. There was no way Lyndon Johnson would keep a Kennedy on as Attorney General. And now you're worried that the publicity for my book will lead back to you. You look old enough to have been involved. No wonder you're scared."

The Don nodded to Scott and said, "Okay."

Thirty-nine

Sara felt her body betraying her, felt it closing down. The shakes, too strong to be called shivers, were wracking her with pain. If the basement cell had a bed she'd feel better, instead of having to cower on the floor. She figured that her near fetal position in one corner of the cell was the best for heat retention but it didn't seem to help much.

She was so cold that her brain had slowed along with her body. Being stripped naked had been humiliating, and she gagged at the memory of the saturated towel pushed on her face. She wasn't sure how long it had gone on, or how many times they'd done it till she passed out, but when Scott finally threw her in the cell he'd said, "You'll soon be ready. You've got tonight to think about it."

She cried and sniveled as she remembered the water filling her throat and nose and thought back to Bush and Cheney's insistence that water boarding was just an enhanced interrogation technique, not torture. Goddamn them. Anyone and his dog could now water board their enemies and justify it by the actions of the US government.

She spat and focused her eyes on a spot on the far wall. If she could concentrate on something else maybe the pain and cold would go away. One brick in the wall had a mark where damp had left a white crystalline stain. She worked on what the shape might be. A butterfly with its wings part opened, a bird, or the shape of a country which she couldn't quite place. Her brain was fooled for three minutes. She thought back to the interrogation, not the greatest memory, but though bad, she had the feeling that Scott hadn't pursued it as vigorously as he might have done. Granted she was cold and miserable in a cell, but he hadn't asked her many more questions. Why not?

    She spent the night in pain, cold, with the shakes, and mental upheaval. She had no way of telling time, the cell was windowless, and she felt she'd been there for days before he came back.

Forty

The Don finished his breakfast of a Denver omelet, pancakes, and fresh orange juice. He'd have coffee later.

A look of distaste crossed his face when Scott came in. He sighed. "Okay, Scott. Let's get her."

They went down to the cell. Scott opened the door and saw Sara cowering in the corner, shivering and still damp.

The Don turned to Scott and said, "What have you done to her, Scott? Help her up and we'll take her out of here. I told you to soften her up, not kill her. She just needed a warning for better behavior in the future. The way she looks now even the men wouldn't want her." He looked at her in disgust. "Have you decided to help us yet, now that you've experienced Scott's hospitality?"

She looked up at him through crusted eyelids. "Get lost!"

The Don turned to Scott.

"Get her fixed up so the so the men will like her." Then he left.

Scott helped her to her feet, feeling her shivering. Her skin was ice cold and she was mumbling, "No...no..."

He dragged her out of the cell and up the stairs to

her bedroom. He wrapped her in a big robe and sat her on the bed while he went to run a shower. As it warmed up he sat by her, even tried to put an arm round her. She flung it off.

Then she heard him say, "Don't worry, you'll be out of here soon."

She looked at him strangely. "What? What do you mean?"

He looked at her and she stared back. Then a call came from downstairs.

"Hurry up with the woman, Scott. We all want a go later…"

"Into the shower," he said. "We'll talk more later."

"Why should I hurry for you animals? What's to talk about?"

"Get in the shower."

Five minutes later he pushed her into the study.

"Sit," the Don said, "and tell."

"Tell what?" she asked.

"You're within one second of going back downstairs," he said. "You are writing this so called novel about JFK's assassination. I want to know the whole background, and where you got your information."

Sara waited. How much could she tell and how much should she hide? The basics were easy. "I got the original idea for the plot when I was crossing the Sierra Nevada from San Francisco to Reno. I'd been on vacation in California and a friend suggested taking a different route and going over Sonora Pass. I was driving up there, kind of in the zone, taking my time…"

"Where the hell are you going with this?'

Scott intervened. "The Don isn't a patient man,

The Woman on the Knoll

Sara. Get a move on."

"Alright. On the way to the pass I drove through this summer vacation area called Kennedy Meadows. The name started me thinking about the assassination. What if there was a second shooter, the sniper on the knoll? But what if, to make it even quirkier, she was a woman? What a great scenario. I had to pull over I was so blown away by the thought. I always have a notebook with me and started writing…"

"Where are those notes?"

"What?" She was surprised by the interruption and lost her train of thought. "Well I guess they might be at my office. I usually keep them as a record, even after I've transcribed them onto my computer."

"And where's that computer now?"

"That's tricky," she said, "I left it with Anji," she said, "but as you know there was a fire there and I don't know what happened to it."

"A fire, huh?"

"You should know. You started it."

"Why would we…never mind that. Tell me why you chose a woman for the second sniper."

"First let's assume there was a second sniper, even though the Warren Commission ruled it out. I thought it would be a great starting point for a novel. So if there is one on the knoll, how would he get away? There were people in the area, but not that close to where spectators thought they saw the puff of smoke. Even so I thought they might have noticed a guy with a long gun. But a woman would be a great alternative. No one would suspect her if she had a baby with her, and the stroller would give her a great way to camouflage a gun holster. So there you go, a perfect scenario, and all my own invention."

"This is crap. I knew all this before."

"You did? Then you must have a great imagination too."

"Okay Scott. Take her back down."

"No! Wait. I'm telling you the truth." Her eyes opened wide and her hands clasped the arms of chair. She thought about the cold and wet, the gasping for breath, and the near drowning she'd endured. "Please, I'm telling you..."

"Scott, take her down."

She tensed as Scott gripped her wrists and ripped her hands off the arms of the chair. She screamed and tried to kick him, but her efforts were feeble after eighteen hours of mistreatment. He pulled her toward the door, opened it and began pushing her down the stairs.

She screamed in fear once more and shouted, "Okay, okay, you bastard! I'll tell you." Scott halted, waiting for the Don to make a decision.

"Okay... But the truth this time," the Don said.

Scott pulled her back up the steps and dumped her in the chair.

She sat there, shaking, and sifting through her brain, trying to separate truth from fiction, a tough job for a novelist. "I received an email from a fan of my books. He didn't give me his name or anything."

"So you have his email address?"

"Sure...on my computer, where d'you think?"

"Shut up with the smart-ass comments. What happened next?"

"We emailed quite a lot."

"I though authors hated fan mail."

"He was enthusiastic about my first novels…"

"Why he? Why d'you think he was a guy?"

Sara stopped. She hadn't thought about a him or a her. "I don't know," she said, "I guess I just assumed…"

"You just assumed…what do you think, Scott?"

"Sounds a bit flaky to me, Boss."

"Yeah. So what happened next?"

"He sent me the idea of the second assassin theory and the woman sniper…"

"That's crap," the Don said. "I've read that authors don't use ideas sent to them."

"I know. The best-selling all authors say that, but I'm not a best-selling author. And the more I checked out the idea the more plausible it seemed. Original, exciting, and on a subject that would fascinate readers. My agent had told me to look for a bigger story. How much bigger could it get? So I starting writing the novel based on the few details in the emails and a lot more imagination and ideas from me."

"How did you get the ideas?"

"How does anyone's brain work? You think of something and let your gray matter kick it around for a few days. Ideas just bubble out."

"Are you being deliberately stupid? Do you want Scott to take you down again?"

Sara looked horrified. "What's wrong? What did I say?"

The Don looked at her disdainfully. "You got a lot more in those emails than you're saying. I'll give you a while to decide to tell me."

"I do not get…"

"Shut up! You've written some other books right?

What about?"

She couldn't see where he was going with this but decided to humor him for now. When he turned the discussion back to the emails she'd be in deep doodoo. "Detective stories and mysteries."

"What are their titles?"

"Sea-saw, Mosaic..."

"Did you get emails suggesting ideas for those books?"

Now she saw where he was going. "No, they were my ideas."

He let her silence brood. "So where are the emails you got sent this time?"

"I already told you. They were on my laptop at Anji's."

"Who's Anji?"

"She's the friend I was staying when the fire..."

"Ah, the fire..."

Sara saw him smile. "You damn near killed her, you bastard!"

The Don smacked her face, rocking her head back. "Don't get mouthy with me! You don't want to make me mad." He sat there mulling over her answers. "Scott?"

"Yes, boss?"

"You got a computer, right?"

"Sure."

"What if you lost it in a fire? What would you do?"

"I'd get my backup data from... Ah..."

Sara had been following this, her eyes flicking from one to the other.

"Okay," the Don said, "where is it?"

Sara started to shake her head. But the Don said,

"Before you say a word, you only get one chance, so get it right."

She swallowed. "I had most of the data on a USB drive."

"Where is it?"

"I..."

"One chance, Jan."

"I kept it in a small fireproof safe at Anji's."

The Donn stared at her then his forehead unwrinkled and he seemed to make a decision. "Scott. Tell Mike to get over there and see what's left in the apartment." He turned back to Jan. "Where was the safe?"

"In the master bedroom...in the closet...it was bolted to the floor."

"And the building security?"

She paused, and the Don pounced. "You better tell me."

"I doubt if there's any now you've torched the place. There used to be an intercom system."

The Don nodded to Scott who left the room.

He turned his attention back to Sara. "Ken Tierney wrote a book about Kennedy. No one took any notice of it but he emailed you with his ideas. Right?"

"No! Who is he?"

"You ever meet him?"

"No."

"Well he mentions you in his files."

"What?"

Sara wondered where this was all going. Then she realized. KT. Ken Tierney. Then she remembered his email, the robbery, and his burglarized files. Now it made sense.

The Don sat back. "So you're an author, Don't

authors have websites? What's the URL of yours?" He got up from his chair and walked over to his computer desk. "You gonna give it to me or do I send you downstairs for more fun and then just Google you anyway?"

Sara's eyes were smarting from his earlier punch. She could feel the shakes coming back and she was tiring fast. No way was she risking the water again.

She told him.

He went quiet as he battled the keyboard with his fat sausage fingers.

"Okay..." He read the first few pages. "Hmm, you were understating your background. Says here that you've written three books, not two like you said."

"Wrong," she said, ignoring the shadow that passed across his face. "I've written five novels, three got published, but my favorites are Mosaic and Sea-Saw, the two I mentioned."

"Okay. So let's get back to The Grassy Knoll. What the hell is going on? Why are you here? What are you investigating?"

"I'm here because you kidnapped me, you dumb bastard."

The Don was on his feet in an instant. He looked at her, a grimace on his face. "Who knows you're here? Are you undercover?"

"Oh yeah, right. I suppose I arranged to be just where you planned to kidnap me, huh?"

This time the Don backhanded her so hard that her neck was jerked round. She heard a click inside her neck, was in agony immediately, and slumped out of her chair.

"Take her back to her room!"

The Woman on the Knoll

Forty-one

Scott entered the Don's study followed by the guy with a beard wearing white Nikes. He was holding a USB drive in his scratched hand.

"Mike finally got it, boss."

"Thanks Mike, take the rest of the day off. Scott, you go get the girl."

Upstairs the guard on the door said to Scott, "So when do we get some fun with her, Scott?"

Scott ignored him and went in. She was curled in her now usual fetal position under the thin sheet. He grabbed her hands and sat her up on the edge of the bed. She whimpered at his touch, tried to stand and as she collapsed against him her thumb brushed against his ear. He pulled her up, put an arm round her waist and half carried her out of the room.

The guard had watched all this and as they passed he put out one hand and grabbed her naked breast and with the other slapped her butt loud enough to get laughs from down below. Scott felt her tense and then start to sob.

The Don looked up as Scott shoved her down onto a swivel desk chair. He shook his head. "What a state you've got yourself into. Even your boyfriend wouldn't want you like this. So now we've exchanged pleasantries, take this." He shoved the keyboard at her. "Put in your password."

Sara hesitated.

The Don hit her, backhanded, on the same part of her face as before. She didn't fall over sideways this time because Scott caught her.

The Don looked at Scott. "Why did you do that?"

"Well, Boss, I figured that if she was too damaged she'd be no use to us."

The Don smiled, then put his face right in Sara's, caressed her flaming red cheek and hissed, "Open up that drive."

"No!"

"Somehow I thought you'd say that. Scott?"

"Yes, Boss."

"Take her down..."

Instead of obeying, Scott bent and whispered in her ear, holding the lobe as he did so. "You might as well logon; you're going to in the end, so save yourself some pain." He stroked the smooth lobe with his fingertips as he let go her ear.

Sara looked past him at the Don.

"Okay...I'll do it." She pulled the laptop closer, hesitated, remembered the force of his slaps, then keyed in the password and watched the data come up.

"That's better," the Don said. "Now show me the emails."

Her fingers flickered over the keyboard and her mail list was displayed on the screen.

"Okay, Scott. You can take her back up now."

Sara's eye flashed with anger. "Do you really think

that removing my website and emails will keep the truth hidden?"

She stopped talking as he slapped her again.

"Take her back up and there's no need to be gentle. Tell the boys they can have her."

Sara stiffened in the chair. "I've done all you asked and now you're..."

"Tough shit, lady. Take her, Scott."

Scott hustled her out of the study and towards the stairs. She fought as much as she could; wedging her elbows and kneecaps into vulnerable spots on his body, but her blows had little impact on him. She was drained of energy. She grabbed hold of the banister but Scott had no trouble breaking her grip. At the top of the stairs the guard was waiting for them, leering even more. Scott pushed her into the room and she collapsed on the bed, shivering.

The guard came straight into the bedroom and grabbed Sara's shoulders. He forced her over on her back and looked at her naked body. He unbelted, unzipped, and dropped his trousers. Sara shivered as she watched him and then looked at Scott. He showed no sign of caring. He just stood there watching. She levered herself up and swung her legs to one side of the bed, but the goon grabbed her and swung her back. He kneeled on the bed and forced her legs apart. Sara looked toward Scott but saw no sympathy.

The goon saw her shudder, heard Scott unzipping and said, "You wait your turn..." Then he laughed and fell down on her, grabbing her wrists. She screamed and tried to bite him but he just banged his head on her forehead. She screamed again, but not so loudly. Then she saw Scott come into her vision at the side of the bed.

She saw and heard him zip up.

The goon heard it as well, paused in his assault, and looked up. Scott pointed two fingers at him. The goon watched and understood moments too late what was about to happen. He tried to roll to the opposite side of the bed but a finger hit him in each eye. Before he could scream Scott stuffed the corner of a pillow into his mouth and punched him hard in the stomach. The breath whooshed out of him. When he hit the floor Scott kicked him in the side of the head. He lay still. Scott grabbed the guard's gun and shot at the window repeatedly. On the fifth attempt it shattered, shards dropping outside.

"Come on!" he shouted at Sara.

The Woman on the Knoll

Forty-two

The Don's people crowded into the room, ignoring the guard's body on the floor.

Mike said, "Everyone outside to search, except you." He pointed at one of the goons. "Stay here and watch out."

"Watch out for what?"

"If I knew that I wouldn't leave you here!"

Mike and the rest ran out. The goon they left behind looked out of the window. Sara crawled out from under the bed, but her foot squeaked on the vinyl flooring. The goon turned and saw her, still naked. He smiled, jumped toward the door and made a grab for her. Scott came out from under the other side of the bed and thumped him at the base of the neck. The noise of him hitting the floor was louder than the blow that felled him. Scott then dragged him across the floor and pushed him out the window.

Sara said, "You've killed him."

"Nah. He's only sleeping."

Sara stared at Scott and opened her mouth ask a hundred questions.

"Who are you?"

"Shush."

She heard such intensity in his low pitched voice that she obeyed. Scott moved toward the door and checked both ways along the landing. Sara draped a sheet around her and followed him.

They froze as they heard footsteps running back into the house downstairs.

"Be quiet and we've got a chance," he said.

He took her hand, led her along the landing, and up the back set of stairs. On the next floor they went back along to the darker end. Sara assumed this was toward the old servants' quarters. Scott paused beneath a trap door set up in the ceiling. He took a short pole from a clip on the wall and reached up. He used the pole to nudge the trapdoor up at one end. There was a click and as the door swung down a set of steps lowered to the floor. He replaced the pole.

"You go up first then I'll follow and deal with the steps. Okay?"

She nodded and went up the steps. Scott averted his gaze as she climbed. When she disappeared in the gloom he followed her up and clicked on the light. He saw where she was balanced on a roof beam and whispered, "Don't move from that spot." He pulled up the steps and as the last rung came up the trapdoor eased closed with a metallic click. He took a small flashlight from a trouser pocket and clicked it on, then killed the attic light.

"Follow me, only step on the beams, be quiet, and don't knock anything over. Think Anne Frank. Okay?"

Sara nodded. This guy had a lot to explain. So far she'd accepted his every lead but that had to stop. She had no idea why he was helping and chances were it was some kind of trap.

Scott went to the far right corner of the attic near some big boxes and waved his hands through immense cobwebs. Then he turned the flashlight around and played the light just ahead of Sara so she could follow his dusty trail. She picked her way across the beams, hanging onto the lowering rafters as she approached. He motioned her in behind the boxes and she saw a space about ten feet by six where the beams were covered in plywood and it looked safe to sit on. She crawled in, went to the far end of the nook, picked up a blanket she found there and wrapped it round her. She heard Scott scrambling over the beams rubbing at the disturbed dust, then he came back and grabbed two cans from a little shelf. He knelt between the boxes and Sara heard pressurized gas being sprayed.

Oh no. She'd escaped all kinds of crap and now this guy was gassing her?

"You bastard!" She leaped toward him.

Forty-three

Scott turned and saw Sara launch herself at him. He punched her back into the hiding place. Sara sprawled on her back panting, her chest hurting, and feeling foolish and angry at the same time. Angry because he'd been so violent and foolish because she could have done a much better job of attacking him.

"What the hell are you doing," he whispered, thrusting his face toward her.

Sara shouted back at him. "What the hell am I doing? What the hell were you doing? Trying to kill…"

Scott grabbed her round the back of the neck with one arm and clamped a hand over her mouth. She squirmed and wriggled and brought her hands up to gouge at his eyes but his arms were longer and he forced her back. Then he pinned her arms and held her down with the weight of his body. He could see her face in the diffused light from the flashlight, her lips pursed and defiance in her eyes.

"Stop it," he hissed at her, "They'll hear us downstairs."

He eased his hand away from her mouth so she could speak.

"What do I care, you were going to kill me anyway."

"Where d'you get that stupid idea?"

"Stupid? I heard the gas."

The crease on Scott's forehead grew as he frowned then he smiled.

"That's quite something," he said. "I was making us safe. Remember all the cobwebs we had to go through to get in here?"

Her turn to frown. "Yes..."

"Guess how I made them?"

Her turn to understand. "Uh...oh...out of a can?"

"You got it. Now do you mind if I finish the job that just might save our lives."

Sara breathed in as his weight disappeared off her chest and she sat up.

"So you were well prepared for this?"

"Yeah. I knew that one day I might need it. And when you arrived I made it a bit bigger. There are some clothes at the back."

She heard the spray again, now finding the sound reassuring and protective. She told him to stay looking the other way and climbed into the sweats. They didn't fit well, but she felt a lot more civilized wearing something. The white Nikes were a perfect size.

"Okay, that should do it," said Scott as he withdrew back into the 'cave' he'd created then switched off the flashlight.

The dark was impenetrable and Sara heard him wriggling back by her. She figured she was safe for the time being. "So what's going on? Who are you?"

"Shush," he said.

She heard the click of the attic hatch followed by the sound of the ladder being pulled down. Some light filtered up into the attic and diffused into their lair. Sara froze.

"You really think they could be up there?"

"Just get up and look around, Mike," the Don said.

She heard footsteps on the rungs and the beam of a flashlight flickered.

"Anything?" called the Don.

"Nah. Nothing but cobwebs. Waste of time. I'm coming back down."

"No. Stay up there and make sure."

They heard a long dramatic sigh and the light beam grew stronger. The footsteps came toward them on the beams they'd recently trod. Sara stiffened as the light grew stronger. Would Mike notice the disturbed dust that Scott had tried to conceal? Was he following their footprints? The footsteps stopped. The beam of the flashlight played around, getting stronger, then weaker.

"Screw it," they heard him mutter. "I hate frickin spiders."

The footsteps grew fainter as did the light. They heard him go down the ladder and then sound of it pushed back up. The hatch banged shut and they were back in darkness.

They stayed there the rest of the day.

Sara asked Scott again and again what was going on, who he was, and why he'd..."

Each time all he'd say was "Shush. Don't make any noise."

She persisted and in the end, worn down by her incessant requests, he said, "They find us they'll kill me, and by the time they finish you'll wish they'd killed you too."

After this stark message and her memories of the last few hours, Sara decided he was right, made herself comfortable on the blanket and surprised herself by falling asleep. She woke feeling cold, and realized the attic wasn't insulated. She saw a faint beam of light and could hear Scott moving around.

She had the sense to keep her voice low. "What are you doing?"

"Ah...hullo sleeping beauty."

"Shut it, Dumbo. What's going on?"

"We're getting out of here."

"How?"

He sounded exasperated. "Do I have to explain everything to you?"

She bounced his words back at him. "Yes. Cos it's both our lives. You said so."

"Can't fault that logic."

He rummaged in a corner of their hideaway and pulled out a thick rope.

"Prepared for everything weren't you?"

His eyes glinted in the flashlight's weakening beam. "Sarcasm won't get you out of here, preparation will. Thus the rope. Happy now?" Scott led her on the teeter totter beam balance again, this time to the ventilation gap at the end of the attic. Sara spent about five minutes rubbing spider webs off her clothes and face while he unscrewed the mesh grill.

"You alright on a rope?" he asked her.

"Will you stop with the with the patronizing questions? Let's get out of here."

He doubled the rope round a rafter and tested the purchase with his weight. Throwing the twin ropes out and down he waved her through first.

"Why not you?"

"Because if I go first and the rope breaks or the beam gives way you'll have no way to come down."

"So I'm the guinea pig to make sure this Jerry rigged escape route works?"

"Whatever. Are you going or not?"

She looked down into pitch blackness. "You're sure it reaches to the ground?"

He shook his head and said, "No." Then he laughed. "You think you've got a choice?"

"Bastard," she whispered, and climbed up on the box he'd placed under the vent.

"Want a hand?" Scott asked and put his hand under her butt.

Sara climbed down off the box, took his hand and bit it, hard. She heard his intake of breath, climbed back up, and swung a leg over the edge. The ropes were under her as she swung round outside the vent and scrabbled with her feet for purchase. She found a small ledge she could stand on, grabbed the ropes and rappelled down, grazing her fingers until she could angle the ropes away from the wall. The ropes did reach the ground so she guessed Scott's preparation had worked.

Scott slithered down after her and then pulled on one end of the rope until it tumbled down. He coiled the rope and then said, "Okay, let's go." and grabbed her hand to lead.

"Let me go and I'll follow," she hissed. But she had some trouble keeping up with him. When they were clear of the house and into the bushes, he stopped to let her catch up.

Before he could complain about her slowness she said, "So where are we going?"

"Away from the house while we can still see it, then we'll head west. There's a stretch of fence there that we should be able to get over..."

"Should? What happened to all the preparations, Mister?"

She could only just see him in the starlight but there was no doubt he was pissed. "Shut up and quit complaining or..."

"Or what?" she hissed back.

"Jeez," he said. "For a start keep your voice down. There are guards all over the place even though I hope they think we're long gone. For all we know they'll shoot on sight. So follow me and this time keep up."

He went more slowly this time and they walked and stumbled through the bushes and trees. She kept up with him as he turned west and the going became easier across a meadow, then they were back into more trees and the uneven ground was littered with pine needles and cones. Unlike in one of Sara's previous books, none of the tree branches overhung the fence, so they couldn't climb across.

"So what next, Maestro?"

"What would you do?"

"What is this? Twenty questions?" Then she realized. "Give me the rope."

She took it from him, selected the most climbable tree near the fence and clambered up to the highest branch that pointed to the fence. She eased along it as far as she felt was safe, tied the rope to it, and dropped the free end to Scott. When she was back on the ground he offered her the free end.

"Oh no, buster. You're going first this time. If you get fried on the electric fence and short it out, I'll be able to get over using your body as a ladder."

"Thanks," he said. "Very funny."

He walked to the fence and pulled the rope tight, then cut it so it would clear the top barbed wire. Then he tied a knot at the end of the rope, walked back to the tree, and climbed up a few feet.

"Keep your feet on the knot like this, hold high up the rope and you'll clear the fence."

"Duh," she said.

Scott let go of the tree, swung down and then up and over the fence. He let go as he arced over clear ground and landed heavily.

"You okay?" Sara asked.

"Yeah...fell on some stones. Your turn."

"How?"

"What do you mean? I showed you."

"But you cut the rope too high for me to reach, Dumbo. I've got to climb back up to the branch to get hold of it."

"Oh yeah, sorry."

Two minutes later she swung over the fence, let go, and landed in a perfect roll.

"Where did you learn that?"

"Parachute school when I got into skydiving."

"Got any other talents?"

"You'd be surprised."

He started to walk away from the fence using his

fading flashlight to show the way.

"Where are we going?"

"There's a gas station about a mile from here."

"You leave a car there for us?"

"No."

"Can we rent one there?"

"No."

She didn't comment but let his answer hang in the air between them. His pace didn't slacken and she dropped behind. "Hang on, "she said.

"Okay. We can go slower…"

"More slowly. Too many people use adjectives for adverbs nowadays."

"What? We're in deep shit and you're correcting my English?"

"Hey, I'm a writer, it's my life."

"Jeez, just follow, will you."

Eventually she saw the glow of the gas station's lights and they crept closer.

"There's no payphone outside," he said.

"So why do you need a payphone?" This guy had been alternately her torturer and her savior. What was he up to now?

"Because I left my cell back in the house."

This time she let him have it. "Prepared huh?"

He ignored her. "Wait here," he said.

She watched from the cover of the trees as he cut across the road and headed for the gloom behind the gas station. Then nothing. For a long time, nothing. Finally a car appeared, lights out, and drove away. She watched it disappear round a corner. He had spent all this time and effort to help her. Why would he steal a car and then leave her behind?

She as still fuming five minutes later when she heard a noise in the brush. She cowered in the dark of a tree trunk. The noises came directly at her so she wriggled around. Then a beam of light skewered her.

Forty-four

"What do you think you're doing?"

Sara heard Scott's voice. "Oh, it's you. What are you doing sneaking up on me like that?"

"You'd prefer I crashed through the bushes? Who the hell else would be out here?"

"How about the garage owner?"

"Yeah well, no one's caught us yet. Let's get going."

"Where?"

Scott looked at her. Sara could just make out his exasperated expression.

"Okay, okay, I'm coming," she said.

He led her parallel to the road just within the trees for a hundred yards. The car was waiting for them, just tucked off the road, no lights on but the engine running. As they got closer she saw it was a nonentity Toyota, perfect for blending into any urban scene.

Sara got in without a word; Scott put it in gear and drove away. They took an hour to reach the nearest town, most of it silence until Sara said, "You're a man of many talents. Who are you really?"

He said nothing until they reached the first traffic

signal on the outskirts of town.

"I'm the person who helped you escape from those cranks," he said.

"Not good enough," she said. "Who do you work for?"

"What do you mean? I was in the family and now I'm on the run from them."

"Well I never believed that crap about the FIA, so are you from the Secret Service?"

He was driving fast now that they were at the outskirts of town. "You're nuts!"

"One more chance to come clean."

He looked across at her again even though he was steering round a tight bend.

"Don't give me that innocent look," she said.

"If I knew what you were talking about I'd help…"

"Liar. You do know what I'm talking about and for some stupid bureaucratic security bullshit reason you're…"

"Enough already. You're too mouthy and a pain in the neck."

"And you were an animal when you had me stretched out on that board and damn near drowned me."

"And saved your precious life. If Mike or the Don had done it you'd still be coughing up lung tissue in that cell. Instead you're free out here."

Sara was silent for the next five miles. He was right of course, she was out of danger…or was she? Maybe this was all some elaborate set up. But they had had her at their mercy. Why would they let Scott help her escape?

"Look, you know all about me," she said. "It's time to talk. Who are you and what's going on? Be honest here, huh?"

"Okay..."

"So what's with all this stuff about the president?"

"Kennedy?"

"No, you idiot. President Uhrquart who's trying to get us out of this war in Iraq and the Don who appears to want to kill him."

"Why would you think the Don wants to murder the president?"

I don't know. Maybe his son was killed in Iraq. Maybe his business is being squeezed like the Mafia's was in 1963. Maybe... who knows, but he's worried about my ideas."

"You're part way there," Scott said. "All I've learned so far is that he's teaming up with another mob to plan it."

"There is a plot?"

"Yeah. But you came along and spoiled everything with your damn book. The Don got sidetracked onto your diversion and I never got further into the conspiracy."

"What do you mean diversion?"

"You set up all this book stuff as a way into his organization, right? Your people used you because of your writing background and concocted this Kennedy plot to draw him out. Who do you work for?"

Sara drew a deep breath. "Of all the stupid ideas..."

"Stop with the stupid," Scott said. "Everything I just said is perfectly logical. Now we need to dump this car. We're leaving an easy trail for the Don to follow and I need to contact my boss. Think about it."

Sara looked across at him. Was he really helping her or tricking her into trusting him? "And which boss is that? The Don?"

"Of course," he said, and looking straight through the windshield he followed up with, "that's why I went to all this pain and trouble to help you."

"Yeah, right."

Scott pulled the car into a motel parking lot in the next small town. With just three motels, two bars and five churches advertised on the sign just outside town limits, Sara thought staying here would be pretty pathetic.

"We're gonna stay here?"

He leaned forward till his head rested on the steering wheel. "I'm not that tired, but I am sick of your whining and bleating. I've helped you without a word of thanks and..."

She smacked him on the cheek.

"What was that for?" he asked looking at her with eyes wide.

"Nothing," Sara said, wondering why she'd hit him. Stress? Uncertainty?

He sat beside her, waiting for an explanation. When none came he said, "Wait here," and opened the door.

"What are you doing?"

"Getting us different wheels," he said.

He disappeared round a corner of the motel.

When he returned she was gone.

Forty-five

Ken Tierney sat on a bench in a local park and flipped open Sara's cell phone. He dialed all the numbers in her directory and got innocuous responses; some literary agents, a couple of publishers, women friends, three police contacts, four no answers and six whothehellareyous.

One number didn't go through. All he got was a number not available message. He tried it three more times. He looked at the number on the screen and didn't recognize the number format as an area code. He stared at it for minutes before the answer hit him. Reverse the digits, bozo.

An older woman's voice answered. "Yes?"

"Hi. Can I speak to Sara please?"

"She's not here at the moment. Can I take a message?"

Ken frowned, what to do next? "Do you know when she'll be back?"

"Who wants to know?"

"This is Special Agent Brown from the FBI's New York bureau."

"How about you leave me a message and a number and I'll see that she calls you back."

Ken sighed. "We need to talk with her urgently. Can I come and see her?"

"I'm not sure when she'll be home."

Damn. The woman must watch those old folk's security warnings on TV. There was way too much distrust nowadays.

"Well what if I came over to see her later this evening?"

"That sounds fine, do you know the address?"

Time for the tricky part.

"Our records seem to be in a mess, Ms....?"

The woman didn't take the hint to give him her name, nor did she offer an address. Instead she said, "Where are you calling from?"

He said, "New York, Queens."

"Then I doubt we'll ever meet," she said, and the line went dead.

"Dammit!"

The Woman on the Knoll

Forty-six

Three years earlier Ken had been driving a country road looking for a house number. He was lost and his GPS was confused by the tree cover. He cruised along, trying to read the way too small house numbers when he saw a guy in the road up ahead. He wouldn't have paid much attention but the guy was hopping up and down, waving at him to stop. In half a second he processed that it was a nice neighborhood, that the guy was well dressed, and that there weren't any nearby bushes that might be hiding muggers or carjackers. He stopped and rolled his window down an inch.

Turned out to be a classic Good Samaritan event. The guy's wife was in labor and his car had stalled. He had just got out when he saw Ken coming, so he hadn't yet tried ringing the bell at one of the gates. Ken did the right thing, getting them to the hospital 30 minutes before the baby was born. They'd named the boy Ken in his honor.

He dialed the number from memory.

"Jerome. How's my Godson?"

"Hey, Ken. He's doing fine. Three years old now and a little terror."

"And Judy?"

"Guess what?" Jerome said. "She's pregnant again, a girl this time."

"Well how about that. When's she due?"

"Two weeks, and before you ask, yes the tank is full."

Ken laughed.

"So why the call after, what is it, six months?"

"Just to hear your voice of course," he said.

The silence hung on the connection between them.

"And...?" Jerome said.

"Well, there is one small thing..."

"Yeah, yeah. You never need a big favor, do you Ken? What is it?"

"Since you insist," Ken said. "I've got a number that I'd like an address on..."

"I bet she's blond and curvy, you old goat,"

Ken thought of Sara, curvy yes, in a slender way, but blonde, nah. "She's more of a brunette," he said.

Jerome chuckled. "How soon?"

"How about now?"

"Aw Ken, Gimme a break."

"Jerome, do I have to remind you how little Ken got to the hospital in time? And the oxygen they gave him...?"

He heard a long sigh. "Okay, give me the number."

The Woman on the Knoll

Forty-seven

Ken rode up the mountain road on his Ducati. Even if he had been able to find a replacement front wheel for the Harley he would still have ridden the Italian superbike for this trip to the mountains. It was faster and quieter, the lightweight frame was much better suited to the twists and turns of the road, and it didn't vibrate the ears off his head.

He passed half a dozen turnoffs and driveways before seeing the sign for 'Harris'. He drove up the well maintained gravel road to an old log cabin with a shady porch on one side and a sunny deck out front. The last of the winter's snow dribbled past two dormer windows on the way to the icicles hanging from the roof. Suddenly Ken realized why mountain cabins didn't have gutters. The snow and ice would wipe them off the eaves. Funny; he'd never thought of that before. He realized he was just sitting on the bike, the engine running and the desmodromic valve system purring its idle, in front of the cabin. He switched the engine off and propped the bike on its stand. As he approached the front door it opened.

"Mrs. Harris?"

No answer. The woman stood there in loose jeans and sweatshirt, a shotgun held across her body from hip to ear. He noticed her hands weren't shaking and her lips were pursed. Eyes narrowed she stared down at him.

"Mrs. Martha Harris?"

"Who's asking?"

My name is Ken, Ken Tierney. I'm looking for Mrs. Harris."

"Yeah, you already said. Why do you want to see her?"

"I think she can help me."

"How?"

"I'll tell her that."

"You will huh? Well you've got to go through me first."

"Why don't you stop playing your little game, Mrs. Harris? We both know who you are. Let's sit down and talk."

Her shotgun came down to horizontal, but still aimed to the side.

"Well, she don't want to talk to you," came a voice from behind him.

Ken looked around. Great! Another old fart with a shotgun. Seemed like the weapon of choice round these parts.

"It's okay, Jake. He's leaving."

"All I want to do is..."

"Get out," the woman said.

Ken paused, then walked around the old man and started the Ducati. Above the rustle of the V-twin, he said, "What about those Kennedys, huh?" and rode away.

He was accelerating slowly through the gate when two shots rang out. Pellets peppered the posts on each side of him and one piece of shot scored a furrow across the top

The Woman on the Knoll

of his right shoulder. He looked in his mirror. The woman was reloading. She'd sent him a message, but what was it? Get out of here? Or?

He braked and then slowly turned. He rode back to the cabin.

The two of them were on the porch now, shotguns angled toward him, but loosely held. They looked at him. He killed the engine and waited.

"Why're you here?" the old man said.

"I told her already."

"So tell me."

"Are you Mr. Harris?

"No. Not that it's your business."

"Then I don't need to talk to you."

That brought the shotgun back up.

Ken waved his hands to show he wasn't holding a gun and said, "All I want to…"

"How d'you find this place?" the man asked.

"Drove up the road."

"You pissant son of a…"

"Jake. Let me handle this," the woman said. "What's your name?"

"I told you, Ken Tierney."

"No. Your real name."

"That is my real name, Goddammit."

"Don't blaspheme, Mr. Tierney. What do you want?"

"You are Mrs. Harris?"

"Depends." Her lips tightened round her mouth.

Ken realized she wouldn't tolerate him for long. He needed something to catch her attention. "Sara's novel," he said.

The woman was good, not a flicker crossed her face, but the man shifted slightly. He knew something, Ken was sure of it.

"I'm coming up on the porch," he said.

"No," they said in unison.

"Tough," he said. He kicked the stand down, propped the bike on it, took off his helmet and rested it on the saddle. Then he took his jacket off and made a slow turn to show he wasn't carrying a gun and walked up to the porch. He sank onto one of the swinging loungers, stretched, and rocked.

"What about Sara?" she said.

Ken rocked. "Can we start over?"

The woman looked at the man. He nodded. They sat opposite him on the other rocker, but not rocking.

"Who are you?" she said. "Not your name again, I got that. But who are you?"

"I had a book published six years ago but it wasn't the bestseller I hoped for."

"Why should we care?" asked the man she'd called Jake.

"Maybe you don't, but it's one reason why I'm here."

"Ken Tierney?" the woman said, and disappeared into the house.

Jake leaned forward and said, "If you so much as touch her I'll kill you. If you even scare her I will hurt you..."

The woman came out of the cabin. "This piece of garbage?" she said, throwing a paperback onto the seat beside him.

Ken saw his own picture staring up at him from the

The Woman on the Knoll

back cover. "Well at least you know I didn't lie about my name."

"So what's your interest here?" she said.

"I'm always interested in people who have my book." The shotgun barrels twitched and he said, "I need to talk to Sara."

"Why?"

"That's for her ears only. So you do know her?"

"I didn't say that."

Ken looked at her. "No, you didn't need to. But you could contact her for me and tell her I need to talk with her."

"Because she's writing a novel about the Kennedy assassination?"

"Exactly."

"And because your book theorized there was a sniper on the knoll? And because she's using a similar plot in her book? What are you going to do? Sue her?"

Ken stifled a smile that he thought she'd find inappropriate. "Not at all. I'm flattered. She's provoked a firestorm of interest and I just think we have some common ground. So can you help me get in touch with her?"

"You've got an email address. Why don't you use that?"

"She's not responding. We exchanged three or four messages but her emails stopped three days ago. I'm worried for her."

Jake and the woman exchanged glances.

"She's perfectly capable of looking after herself."

Bingo. The first crack in the wall. "I'm aware of that, but we had a meeting arranged and she never showed up."

Another glance between the two of them.

"Your book," Jake said. "You make that stuff up? Or you got any proof?"

"No one who's ever written about the assassination has enough proof." Ken saw that Jake was about to cut in and headed him off. "But there were enough eye witnesses and circumstantial evidence to show that a sniper could have been on the grassy knoll."

"Yeah, I read that. But nobody's made a film of your book, have they?" He emphasized the 'your' in your book.

"You're right. Oliver Stone never called me. Probably because my book doesn't have any huge revelations - just an analysis that postulated a 'what if'."

"What made you write your book, Ken?" Martha asked.

"It started as a hobby but then it just took me over. When I'd gathered a huge amount of information and had a few ideas I thought I'd do something creative. If you've read my book, you'll know why I want to meet this novelist whose plot is so similar to my theory."

Martha leaned forward. "Ken, you seem like a decent guy, and while the ideas in the two books seem similar, I'm having a hard time seeing how Sara's novel could help you. I'm even more curious about how you found out I live here."

"Like I said, Sara and I exchanged a lot of emails and we were going to meet here one day."

"Liar!" said Jake. "She'd never have told you about this cabin."

Ken knew this was the weak area of his story, but thought he had it covered pretty well. "No, it's true. We were going to get together here but we hadn't set a date yet. I was concerned that I hadn't heard from her so I came anyway."

"Why didn't you say that at first?"

"Because I had no idea how much she confides in you. Who are you guys, anyway?"

Martha and Jake exchanged glances.

He said, "Friends of the family."

"What family?" asked Ken.

"Uh-uh. You're the one who came here looking for information, but it's us asking the questions. You don't get Jack until you check out."

Ken sat forward and opened his mouth to speak.

"No. You be quiet," said Jake. "Prove who you are."

"Hell, you've got a copy of my book, and like Sara my picture's on the back cover. What more do you want?"

"What other books have you written?"

"None."

"Newspaper, magazine articles?"

"None, but…"

"Website, blog, any social networking?"

"No…"

"Now here's where I have a problem, Ken. If this hobby of yours is so all-consuming, why haven't you done any of those things?"

Ken reflected on how much to tell these people. He thought they were sincere but he didn't know how much Sara might have told them.

"I preferred to publish my ideas in one place rather than piecemeal."

"And what reaction did your book get?" asked

Martha.

"Mainly criticism that what the witnesses saw and heard could be explained by other phenomena. Reflections, grainy photographs, echoes, people running in fear rather than up the knoll toward a gunman. So why are you so interested in my book?"

Then a voice from the door behind him said, "Because, as you have guessed, I used some of your information in my novel."

Forty-eight

"Sara!" shouted Martha. "Why didn't you tell us you were coming? Oh it's so good to see you. Jake, look who's here."

"I can see for myself, Martha, and she don't look a day older than when I first met her."

Hugs all round.

Sara looked at Ken and said, "What's he doing here?"

Ken had stood to shake hands but he grasped at air as she recoiled from him.

"What's he been saying? Did he tell you about chasing me after the fire at Anji's apartment? And about knocking out a friendly taxi driver in my hotel room?"

Ken tried to defuse the situation by sitting back down on the slider. Jake, Martha, and Sara stood in a semicircle facing him.

"I'm getting my shotgun," Jake said, disappearing into the cabin.

"No need for that," Ken said. "I can explain everything. Let's start with the emails."

"What emails?"

"I'm KT, Ken Tierney. The emails we exchanged to

set up a meeting in that café. I waited outside. I wanted to trust you, but after my office was broken into, and your novel matched my theory so closely, I decided to follow you to make sure you weren't part of another conspiracy."

"What?"

"How could I know?" said Ken. "So I followed your taxi and joined the crowd when you went to check on the burning apartment. In the crush I lost sight of you. Then I called…"

Jake came out of the cabin brandishing his pump-action and racked a round. "Okay you sumbitch…"

"Jake, don't you go shooting anyone. We'll hear his story first then you can shoot him," said Martha. "Carry on young man."

"I'm not happy about guns being pointed at me," he said.

Jake let the barrel droop a couple inches toward the deck. "That's okay," said Jake. "I don't mind. Get on with it."

Ken looked back at Sara. "When I saw you in the crowd I tried to reach you. I called your name but you turned and ran. I didn't know why, until I saw a guy with white Nikes chasing…" He stopped as he saw her shoes.

"Keep going," Jake said.

"He was chasing you and tried to grab your taxi. I jumped on him and you roared off. I followed on my Harley, waited at the hospital while you went in and then followed you to the hotel. I really needed to speak with you."

"Why?"

"Can I finish explaining what happened?"

"If you must," she said, sitting opposite him.

"I booked a room in the hotel and heard what number you were in. I came to your door about 20 minutes later assuming the taxi driver had left. But as I got there he opened the door in my face, and before I knew it I'd hit him. I needed to speak to you so I dragged him into the bathroom, but you woke up and ran for it when you heard the noise I made. All I wanted to do was talk."

"I don't believe you," said Jake. "People don't go round hitting folks for nothing."

"But they sometimes point shotguns at people," Ken said.

Jake grunted.

"Go on Ken," Sara said, "tell us what was so important that you had to see me?"

"Because some parts of your plot ring true."

"Like what?"

"I tracked down a rumor of a stroller being seen. Then there are photos of shadowy figures by the fence on the knoll. Some have been exposed as fakes, but some haven't. Not yet. So you either have a fertile imagination or a source with inside information."

"That's enough," said Jake. "Are you implying that this girl I've known for thirty years is involved in some…?"

"Jake!" Martha interrupted. "I think Mr. Tierney here still has more to tell us. What else is there? And if you have the time and money to fund this 'hobby' what do you do in the real world? Or are you with the Secret Service? The CIA?"

Ken laughed.

"Don't be disrespectful," said Jake, gesturing with the shotgun.

"No, of course not, but it is just a hobby. Robert

Kennedy's assassination was also too cut and dried, and another bungled investigation with another patsy. I've always thought that if the truth of JFK's assassination could be discovered that we'd be halfway to solving RFK's as well. There are too many unanswered questions and too many unexplained issues."

"Like what?" said Jake.

"Like finding the missing bullet on Governor Connolly's stretcher. Whether Oswald was good enough to shoot accurately in the time he had. Why he didn't fire when he had an easier angle before the motorcade turned left onto Elm. Why the discrepancies on how many shots were fired. Why there were two shell casings and one live round on the 6th floor of the Texas school depository. Whether there was a shooter on the DalTex building roof. Was there a shooter on the knoll?"

"So who pays you? Who do you work for?" asked Martha.

"No one. I can afford this myself. I go to all the conferences, participate in the online discussions and user groups, Facebook groups, alt.kennedy.com and so on. It's my passion."

"You expect us to believe that?" Jake said. "Martha, let me have him for five minutes and I'll get him talking. The Koreans taught us a thing or two in 1959."

"I don't think so, Jake. Let's wrap this up for tonight and we can continue in the morning. Ken, I'm assuming you'll accept an invitation to stay with us?"

Jake smiled at Ken and twitched the barrel of his gun.

Ken said, "That would be most generous."

"Don't you be sarcastic with me, young man. And

come morning we better get the full story out of you. Think on that."

Jake led him into the cabin.

Martha went to follow but Sara touched her arm. "Wait a minute. I called you and left a message for you to go to Jake's. Why are you still here?"

"I did go to his place. I stayed for two nights but nothing happened so I came home."

Sara sighed. "Oh Grandma..."

"What? I should leave here forever?"

"It's just that it might be dangerous. We should go back to Jake's tomorrow."

Forty-nine

Jake didn't sleep too well. His bed was a rocker in the hallway outside Ken's bedroom door. He didn't trust the stranger not to sneak away during the night, regardless of his 'passion for all things JFK'.

But when he heard the warning cans rattle on the front porch at 5 am he had to go down to check. That damn cinnamon bear just would not give up and kept knocking the trip wire. Martha never left trash out nor any ground floor windows open, but the bear kept prowling around. He looked out the kitchen window and there she was, snurfling along the porch in the weak moonlight. He'd first seen her as a cub two years before, and she was a solid teenager now, always getting into trouble. Martha even had to bring in the bird feeders every night or she'd swat them down and crack the plastic to get at the seeds. He watched her as she ambled back into the forest.

"Everything alright, Jake?"

He jumped at the sound of Sara's voice. He turned to talk to her, but as his gaze traversed the trees he saw movement. And it wasn't the bear. She'd gone the other direction.

"Jake, what's the...?"

The Woman on the Knoll

"Come tell me what you see out here, Sara."

She moved alongside him and peered out. She scanned back and forth but all she saw was trees.

"Nothing," she said. "What do you...?"

"Keep watching."

"Jake?"

"Just keep watching..."

"Aaaah."

"You see it?"

"Yeah. Someone's hiding just inside the tree line."

"You keep an eye out here and I'll check the back."

Jake turned and knocked into Ken who'd just come downstairs.

"Goddammit! Get outa my way."

"Sorry, Jake," Ken said.

Jake stopped in his tracks. "So is the guy out front a friend of yours?"

"What? What guy?" Ken's ingenuous expression seemed to reassure Jake.

"Oh, never mind. But since you're here you can do something useful. Go check the back while I go wake Martha."

Ken went through and peered at the gloom through the kitchen window. He narrowed his eyes and scanned from left to right. Then again. And again. On the fourth pass he saw a difference. On the left, a branch had moved downwards, as though someone had leaned against it.

He resumed his watch and on the twelfth pass he saw the small huff of an exhalation in the cold mountain air, to the right this time. He heard a soft noise behind him and turned to see Jake and Martha.

"What you got out there?" said Jake.

"Two definite, don't know how many more."

"Who are they?" said Martha.

"They're with you, aren't they?" Jake said to Ken, sounding suspicious again.

"Don't be stupid, Jake. If they were they'd have come before now. Why don't you ask Sara?"

"Why her?"

"Shit, shit, shit!"

They all turned as Sara came into the room. "There's three coming up the drive, Jake. Two went either side of the gate and the third is almost at the porch."

"I'll sort him out," said Jake. "You keep a lookout back here. Don't want them creeping up behind us."

Jake walked toward the front door.

Sara said, "Martha, are your guns still in the safe?"

"All except my shotgun, darling. That's right here."

"Can you shoot, Ken?"

"Can a Marine piss in the dark?"

Sara threw open a cupboard door and pulled on the third shelf. There was a click and the shelves opened out to reveal a gun locker behind. She unlocked it revealing a semi-automatic and a rifle. One place in the rack was empty.

"The pistol's mine," she said, picking it up with its shoulder holster. "You can take the Winchester."

She passed it to him with a box of ammo. "You better load it."

He checked the clip and the bolt action. "Is this old thing any good?"

She turned and said, "I've been hunting with it since I was twelve. It's been regularly cleaned, and it's

The Woman on the Knoll

accurate. What more do you want?"

"Okay, sorry. Do you have another hand gun in the drawer?" He pointed to the bottom of the cabinet.

"No," Sara said, and closed the door as he reached for the handle. She locked the door, swung the shelves into place, and led him back into the kitchen. From there they could watch the back and also keep an eye on Jake behind them. He was standing in the doorway looking out over the front porch, his shotgun cradled across his chest. In front of him was a guy poised with his foot on the first step.

"That's far enough."

Sara looked past Jake. The guy was dressed in jeans and a brown leather jacket, his arms held away from his body, palms facing toward Jake. Sara laughed as she saw the raw scratches on his nose and hands.

Ken was at her side. "Do you know him?"

"Yeah, his name's Mike. How about you?"

"I saw him in the crowd outside the apartment fire and then he chased your taxi. I left him with a bad case of road rash."

"Yeah, I saw you both. So how did he find us?" she said.

"I don't know. You stay here, I'll go help Jake."

"What do you want?" Jake said, looking down on the man.

Ken joined Jake on the porch and scanned to both sides to try and see the other two men Sara had mentioned. There was only one and he was monitoring Jake and Mike's conversation.

"I just want to talk to Sara."

"She ain't here."

Mike let his hands fall to his side.

"Don't even think about that bulge in your jacket," said Jake, raising the shotgun from its relaxed position.

"I told you, I just want to talk."

"Who are you?"

"A friend of Sara's."

"Get outa here."

"We need to talk to her." His voice had a hard edge.

"She's not here," said Jake, now pointing the barrel at the visitor.

"Okay, if you say so." He turned and walked halfway to the gate, then looked back. "You only get this one chance..."

"Git!"

Mike shook his head and walked on.

Jake came into the cabin and closed the door. "What now?" he called through to Sara.

"I've got a lot to tell you, but there's no time. I don't know how they found us but we need to lose them."

Jake and Martha moved toward the kitchen.

Ken said, "How we going to do that?" Then he paused and said, "What's that smell? Did someone light the wood stove?"

"No. We haven't used it since June."

Ken saw wisps of smoke wafting across the kitchen window, and then flames licking up the side of the cabin. "Goddammit Sara. You were watching back here. Didn't you notice the stink?"

"Don't blaspheme my grand-daughter, young man. And anyway, she's anosmic."

"What?"

"She's had no sense of smell since she was born."

"Well she doesn't need it now either. We can all see the way those flames are growing."

"Will you stop talking as though I'm not here," said Sara.

"Sorry," said Ken. "So what are we going to do? I don't think the front door is going to be an option. Maybe if we go upstairs... no, it's too high to... what are you doing?"

Sara, Martha, and Jake were moving the kitchen table off the rug. There was just room to put it to one side.

"Just follow us," Sara said.

Jake pulled up the rug revealing a trapdoor. He and Martha went down the steps.

"What we going to do, hide in the cellar?"

Sara said, "Shut up, Ken and get down there."

"We'll be trapped."

"No we won't, but you can suit yourself," she said. "We're going."

She followed Jake and Martha then looked back up the steps. "You coming?"

Ken heard the roar of a large diesel truck outside, the noise getting louder. Automatic weapons fire crackled as the truck crashed into the front of the building, the floor jolting under his feet. Bullets whistled high through the kitchen. As he dived for the hole in the floor he hoped that whoever was outside wanted them alive, but he wasn't convinced. He knelt near the top of the steps to pull the trapdoor closed, but Sara shouted, "Leave it," grabbed his hand and pulled him down the last few steps and across the cellar to a door.

"What...? If we leave the trapdoor open they'll know we came down here."

"So what. Come down. Now!"

Duncan King

He did.

Fifty

Sara pushed Ken across the cellar to where Jake was leaning out of a passageway. He hauled Ken through. Sara followed, then slammed and bolted the door behind her. In the light of Martha's flashlight she knocked on the door. "Solid steel, Ken. They'll take a while to get through."

He looked round from the door, realizing they were in a low passageway, with wood framing supporting up the roof.

"How...?"

"Be quiet," said Martha. "Follow me."

Since she had the only light, he did, keeping his head low after the first time he cracked it against a wooden beam. Then he tripped over a coil of blackened metal tubing.

"Shit! What is this place?" he whispered to Jake behind him.

"We figure the original owners were running moonshine. During Prohibition they probably used this tunnel for storage as well as an escape route from the cabin."

Ken reckoned they'd gone a hundred feet when Martha stopped and her light showed another steel door.

She unbolted it and peered around. The tunnel ran another few feet and ended in a steel grill secured with a huge padlock. She unlocked it with an equally large key and they all passed through. She relocked the grill and they moved through the trees, heading uphill. Looking back Ken saw that the grill had a danger sign with a poison symbol.

He didn't need to be told to be quiet now. They were close to where he'd seen the huffed breaths in the trees. He assumed the guy had gone toward the cabin to set light to it, but couldn't be sure. Shouts were coming from the cabin now, but the noise was dying down.

"This way," whispered Martha, taking a trail that angled away from the cabin. For an old woman she set a fearsome pace. His town clothes were getting snagged by the thorny brush and his shoes kept slipping on the dusty trail. He held the rifle up so it didn't catch against any branches. After a mile she paused and held a finger to her lips. Ken was panting so hard he couldn't hear a thing. Apparently Martha seemed satisfied, because she set a slower pace on up the mountain.

After another ten minutes she paused again. She shook her head and looked at Jake and Sara. They confirmed a lack of pursuit with affirmative nods.

Ken looked at Sara and said, "What…?"

"Shush", all three whispered.

Jake took point and led them on through the forest. He kept going uphill though. Ken didn't understand why. Surely they needed to get off the mountain. Then they heard the diesel truck. The engine noise was coming in their direction.

They heard it stop. Raised voices came from about a hundred yards away.

The Woman on the Knoll

"Shit. How do they know we're here?" Sara said.

Ken gazed at her in understanding. "They also followed you to the cabin."

Her eyes widened. "What do you...? Hey!" she said in an outraged whisper as Ken ran his hands over her body. "Gettoff!"

Jake raised his shotgun but Martha slapped it down. When Ken had finished running his hands over Sara he ruffled her hair and felt her head. Then he sat her down and pulled off one of her shoes. Finally Sara understood. She grabbed the other and started probing it with her fingers. She bent the sole up and then down, glimpsing a small crack in the insole.

"That goddammed Scott."

"Sara!" said Martha.

"Sorry, Grandma."

She passed the shoe to Ken who used more pressure to open the crack, and he saw a small device buried in there. She nodded, put the good shoe back on, took the offending one back, and led them all to the left, away from the trail. When they'd gone about 300 yards they came to a clearing in the trees. Sara went to a cliff edge above a ravine and threw the shoe as far as she could. Then she led them to the right, away from the cliff and uphill through the trees. Their delay in going to the cliff meant that their pursuers' voices were louder now. Ken saw movement to his right and fell to the ground, grabbing Sara's bare foot as he did. She tumbled and looked back at him, but it was his turn to hold a finger to his lips. She nodded. Jake and Martha sensed something and they froze near some trees.

The voices came even closer and Sara recognized

Scott's saying, "Further to the west..." before the noises became less distinct and then faded.

They unfroze and resumed walking through the pines, Sara hobbling as pine cones and stones dug into her bare foot.

"Let's get their truck," Jake said. "If we keep going up they'll surround us at the top."

"But there's cell coverage at the summit, Jake. We can call for help."

"I dunno, reception can be patchy. I say we grab their wheels and get away."

Sara looked at Ken. "What do you think?"

"I'm with Jake," he said. "Those guys are going to be a while getting down into the canyon and finding your shoe."

"And you think they left the keys in the truck for us?"

"Martha, it's all downhill once we turn the sucker around. We'll just roll into town."

Jake led the way, angling back to where they'd first heard the voices. They soon hit the edge of the road, emerging about fifty yards downhill from the truck. Jake crept through the undergrowth toward it in case there was a guard while Sara and Martha kept watch. Jake was right alongside the truck before they dared follow him. Jake reached up and grabbed the passenger side handle. He pulled the door open and swung up, only to fall back as a shot came from the driver's side.

"No!" cried Martha who ran up firing her shotgun, the shots booming as she splattered the gunman in the driver's seat.

Sara knelt by Jake's body. There was no blood

pulsing from his head. Martha wailed and threw herself at him but Ken grabbed her. "We have to get out of here. They'll be back soon."

Martha continued howling.

Sara said, "Let's get the truck turned around and…"

"No time," Ken shouted, "we need to run for it."

"We have to take the truck," Sara yelled. "They'll soon catch up if we leave it."

She ran round to the driver's door and hauled the driver's corpse out. She jumped up into the cab, and gagging, threw a mangled arm onto the road.

"The brake's off, push this sucker backwards." Ken let Martha sag by Jake and ran to the front of the truck. Sara already had it rolling backwards on the hill and Ken leaned against it adding more momentum. Sara hauled the wheel over once she thought the truck was rolling fast enough, and Ken ran back to Martha, pulled her up and then helped her along the road. Sara had pulled the truck around about 120 degrees and was fighting the manual steering to turn it downhill but it was rolling way too slowly. Ken pushed Martha up into the cab, then ran to the rear of the truck and pushed as hard as he could. When Sara managed to straighten the truck so it pointed downhill, Ken ran to the front and jumped into the cab himself, pushing Martha into the middle of the bench seat.

"God! Are you OK?" Ken said.

Sara was covered in blood and spitting.

"Yeah. The driver was still gushing when I pulled him out." She spat again. The truck gathered speed as it swayed down the road. "We've got 15 miles of downhill to go, no power steering and no power brakes, but luckily the truck's too old to have a steering lock." she said. "I think we've got a chance."

Ken looked at Martha between them. She seemed to have pulled herself together and was reloading her shotgun. Ken saw the look in her eyes and was glad he wouldn't be looking down the barrels.

They were gathering speed down the hill now and Sara was having an easier time with the steering until a fusillade of shots rang out. Ken felt the truck lurch and was worried that Sara was hit until he saw she was fighting the wheel.

"Must be one of the tires," she shouted. "I can't hold it!"

Ken lunged across Martha to help Sara as more shots peppered the truck. As he grabbed the steering wheel it jerked violently and they careened off the road into the trees. Bushes and branches scrubbed the sides, and slowed them so that when a pine tree stopped them dead they were shaken but not injured.

They scrambled out of the cab as quickly as possible. Martha fell over and Ken helped Sara lift her from the ground. They hurried farther into the trees. Martha slowed them down so when they came to a large felled tree they hunkered behind it. As a defensive position it sucked but would have to do. Ken saw that Sara had her pistol out and ready to fire but then he noticed that the shotgun was lying on the forest floor 25 yards behind them. He ran and retrieved it and when he was back behind the log he expected Sara to say something, but not, "Where's the rifle?"

Fifty-one

Shit! Where was the rifle?

Ken thought furiously.

"I must have dropped it when I was pushing the truck. Goddammit!"

"Don't swear," Sara said automatically.

"We should get moving again," Ken said.

"She can't," said Sara, pointing at Martha's ankle. Blood was flowing from it. Sara pulled the lace from her remaining sneaker and tightened it to Martha's leg above the injury.

Martha stopped sobbing and then started laughing hysterically. Sara put her arms around her and whispered urgently into her ear. "Grandma, you have to be quiet. They might hear us."

No reaction. If anything Martha got even louder. Sara looked at Ken, realized he couldn't help and slapped Martha hard. Martha crumpled, whimpering, and Sara stared at her, horror stricken at what she'd done. "I've never hit her before, never..."

Ken couldn't lose Sara to emotion as well so he said, "Who are those guys?"

Sara's face cleared and then Ken saw the lines on

her face harden.

"I only met two of them. Mike you saw at the fire and Scott rescued me from the Don's house…"

"What?"

"Doesn't matter. Scott told me he was with the FIA…"

"Who?"

"The FIA. Federal Investigation Agency. He said they were part of Homeland Security and that he'd take me to a safe house."

"I've never heard of the FIA."

"Probably because they don't exist. Anyway the safe house turned out to be a headquarters for organized crime. They held me there for a couple of days trying to find out more about my book and where I got the plot details from. It wasn't fun. They must have put that tracker in my shoe, and then let Scott help me escape. It was realistic too. Scott even threw one guy out of a second floor window." She paused and looked at him. "So what's your real story?"

"It's a long and…"

"We've might have the time," she said, checking over the log.

"You think?"

"Yeah. I don't hear them."

Ken paused gathering his thoughts. "About 50 years ago my father was one of Bobby Kennedy's staff…"

"What?"

"Will you just listen?"

She nodded.

"Dad worked for him from 1962 on. Bobby was Attorney General and starting his war on organized crime.

The Woman on the Knoll

He employed Dad as a researcher gathering information on organized crime and trade union corruption for the upcoming Senate inquiries. When JFK was killed Bobby was distraught and overcome with grief. Jack was everything to him and he believed that he'd been assassinated because of the investigations. He was also angry and scared."

"Scared of being next?"

"Not just that. He and JFK had been secretly encouraging another Cuban insurrection. After the assassination he was scared that it might become public knowledge if the investigation got too close to him."

"You mean if the Warren Commission found out? Are you serious?"

"Sure. If it came to light then the Kennedy myth would have vaporized. Bobby also wondered whether the Cubans might have discovered the plans for the invasion. He and Jack had plotted with the CIA for years to kill Castro. Maybe Fidel could have set up the assassination. Either way, if it was the mob or Castro, Bobby felt to blame. Ironically, as Attorney General, Hoover and the FBI reported to him, but within hours it was obvious that everyone wanted to believe that Oswald was the lone gunman.

"Bobby's other problem was that he was going to lose his job and his power base. Lyndon Johnson was now president, and he'd want to appoint his own Attorney General. Bobby would have no say in the investigation and he didn't believe the Warren Commission would get at the truth so in January 1964, he made dad an offer he couldn't refuse."

"What?"

"He wanted a private investigation; he didn't trust Hoover, the Dallas police were sloppy, and the Secret Service were bound to cover their asses."

"So what happened?"

"Bobby got him accredited as an independent reporter and dad interviewed everyone he could find. He visited all the scenes, the Book Depository, Dealey Plaza, the Texas Theater in Oak Cliff, Oswald's house, the grassy knoll and so on. He created a huge file of information. And at the end Bobby accepted his conclusions, although he had no proof."

"And...?" said Sara.

"He believed that there was a conspiracy; that the mafia was behind the shooting, and that there was a shooter on the grassy knoll. Dad was kind of torqued out about the whole thing because Bobby felt even worse when he told him. Bobby thought his pursuit of the mob through the courts had precipitated his brother's death and went into total grief for months. When the Warren Commission offered to meet him before publication of their report he couldn't face it, so he sent Teddy instead. Teddy accepted their conclusion that there was a single gunman, and in public Bobby did too. But he went to his grave, five years later, still believing my dad's version."

"And you're still working on this after all these years?" she said.

"This is confidential, right?"

Sara laughed. "We're gonna be dead in an hour. Who cares?"

Ken took another look over the log. "For the next five years until he was also assassinated, Bobby had dad on a retainer to keep digging. He followed up every lead,

The Woman on the Knoll

every crackpot conspiracy theory, every new rumor in the press, and reported monthly to Bobby."

"So what happened when Bobby was assassinated?"

Ken looked at her. "After he was killed, Teddy, Edward Kennedy that is, found the reports that Dad had sent to Bobby. Teddy didn't doubt the Warren Commissions findings, but he did have concerns about Bobby's death. So he kept Dad on as investigator, looking into both his brothers' assassinations. The retainer diminished over the years but until Teddy died, Dad, and then I, gave him reports on our progress."

"Did you find anything new?" asked Sara.

"A few things, small inconsistencies, and we, now I, have a few hypotheses that we could check out if anyone from that time ever talks. The problem now is that everyone from that time is dying. Maybe there will be a deathbed confession one day, but who knows?"

"Put down your weapon, Sara. You too, Tierney."

The Don stood behind them, gun in hand.

Fifty-two

Sara whirled around to face the threat, then heard two other guns being cocked. The Don, Mike, and Scott had crept up behind them. She slowed and let the pistol fall at her feet. Martha looked up, gasped, went rigid in Ken's arms and collapsed. He kept hold of her.

The Don said to Ken, "Push the shotgun away with your foot."

He did.

"Sara, back away from your gun."

Sara obeyed. Ken saw her eyes blazing in fury and worried that she'd do something stupid. Then another two men appeared and the moment passed. He felt his arms being grabbed.

"Did you really think you could get away from me, Sara?" the Don asked.

She spat at him, but missed.

He laughed at her. "And you hooked up with Ken, huh? New boyfriend is he?"

She ignored him, and then shrieked as her arm was twisted behind her.

"Answer the man!"

"He's not my boyfriend," said Sara.

The Woman on the Knoll

"No, he's the Ken Tierney who wrote the Kennedy book, isn't he? The book you stole some of your ideas from, or was it the other way round." He laughed. "Okay, let's get them back to the road. Mike, you go on ahead and make sure no one came by to check on the gunshots. You," he pointed at Ken, "carry the old lady. Let's go!"

"Is she okay, Ken?" Sara asked, as he lifted Martha up.

"I think so," he said, "she just…"

"Shut up and walk!" the Don shouted.

"Who's your friend, Sara?" Ken said.

"I said, shut up!"

Sara ignored him. "They call him the Don. He's a sadistic son of a…" She stopped as the Don stepped forward and smacked her on the side of the face. Ken watched her fall but carrying Martha, he couldn't do much to help her.

"Get up and keep walking!"

Sara wiped blood off her face, stared defiantly at the Don, and then limped toward the road. He laughed when she stumbled as a sharp stone cut into her foot. When they reached the road, Scott had started the truck, backed it out of the trees, and was putting on the spare.

Scott called, "All clear, no one on the road."

The Don looked around and smiled.

"OK, put the old woman in the back," he said to Ken, "and you two," he pointed to a couple of his men, "Bring Sara and Ken up here. Scott, when you're done with the tire, reverse the truck up here."

The armed men shepherded Ken and Sara behind the Don as he strode back up to the bodies on the road. The blood on Jake's head was already attracting flies.

"Okay," the Don said to Ken and Sara, "pick him up and take him into the trees over there."

"No!" said Sara. "Do it yourself."

The Don nodded to one of the guards who struck her with the butt of his gun. She screamed and fell, clutching her side below the ribs, a sickening kidney hit.

"Okay, Tierney. You do it. Now."

Ken took a step towards him and then stopped when the Don pointed his pistol at Sara. He lifted Jake as carefully as possible; cradling his smashed head in the crook of his arm, and carried him through the first few trees at the edge of the road.

"Okay. Drop him down there."

Ken lowered the old man's body to the ground.

"Leave him there. Now go get Jim."

"Who?"

The guy you blasted in the truck. His body's on the other side of the road. We'll leave the two of them here with their shotguns, all neat and tidy."

Ken led the way back to the road as Scott reversed the truck to where they were all standing. He got out and joined the group, making four armed men, the Don, Sara and Ken.

The Don pushed Ken and said, "I said, go get Jim."

Before Ken could move, they heard Martha shout from the back of the truck, her voice not so feeble now, "David!"

The Don's head whipped around, his face contorted. "What?" He saw Martha and laughed at her until she brought up the rifle she'd been hiding behind the tailgate. He stopped laughing when Martha shot him.

Now Ken remembered where he'd put the old rifle

when he was pushing the truck.

The Don, David as Martha had called him, collapsed on the ground holding his leg. Blood spurted between his fingers. After his first scream he shouted at Martha, "You old hag. I should have left you on the streets where I found you."

Scott and the other men overcame their shock and fired at Martha who ducked behind the tailgate. The truck was an old Unimog, a Mercedes military vehicle that had once been a troop carrier in Afghanistan. The quarter inch steel of the tailgate easily resisted the rounds they were firing.

Ken and Sara were forgotten in the noise and furious gunfire and Ken dived for the pistol that the Don had dropped. As the firing slackened he shouted, "Drop your guns!"

They all looked around and saw him holding the barrel against the Don's head. He nodded. All dropped their weapons except Scott on the right who raised his to fire. Ken didn't see the movement as he concentrated on the three men to his left. Sara's warning cry was silenced by another crack of the rifle from the back of the truck. Scott dropped without a sound.

"You others, down on your faces! Now."

Martha's face was pale, but the venom in her voice flattened them instantly. "Ken. Watch over them and shoot if they move."

Sara ran to the back of the truck and lowered the tailgate. She took the time to release the tourniquet to let blood flow round Martha's foot before tightening it again, and then helped Martha down. "Are sure you're alright, Grandma?"

"Hush child, of course I am."

"But you just shot two people…"

"And not for the first time. As you know."

Martha walked toward the Don and aimed her rifle at his face from ten feet. "You bastard. All these years. All that wasted grief and sorrow. All the running and hiding. I'm going to…"

"Grandma, don't," shouted Sara, as she saw Martha's finger tighten on the trigger.

"Do you know who this is?" Martha shouted.

"Yes. He's the Don. His people tortured me for two days before I escaped from the house. He was frantic to find out more about my book."

Martha smiled. "I said it would work. We flushed him out. But his hair is white now; it used to be blond."

Ken tried to understand what she meant.

"They were bound to get scared when the truth started to circulate, even if it was in a so-called novel."

Ken tried to get his head round all this new information but there were too many threads.

"But what you don't know girl, is that this is bastard is your Grandfather."

"My…" stuttered Sara.

Ken watched, amazed. What the hell was going on here?

"Ken, meet the architect of JFK's assassination, my old boyfriend, David. You remember in Sara's novel how the sniper on the grassy knoll was forced there by her boyfriend's kidnapping and torture. This is the boyfriend."

"Jan, please…let me explain…" the Don whimpered.

"Shut up. And my name is Martha now. For over

The Woman on the Knoll

50 years I have lived with the thought that you were dead because of me. I was chased halfway round the world and I only kept going because of our son and then our grand-daughter. And you engineered the whole plot. Gullible little old me, huh? Well screw you, David."

"Son? Grand-daughter? What are you talking about?" said the Don.

"Grandma?"

"What is it, Sara?"

"Are you sure it's him?"

"What's your name, David?"

"David Altini," he confirmed.

"Did you realize you were torturing your own grand-daughter?"

"I didn't even know I had a child."

"You don't any more. He died when Sara was four. I've been her closest family ever since."

The Don, David, groaned. "But you never had a child when…"

"When you chased and tried to have me killed, in Maine, and on the island? Damn right I didn't. I knew you guys would never give up and he wouldn't be safe. After David was born, and yes Goddammit, I named him after you, my sister raised him, even though it broke up her marriage. He was a good kid, did well at college and had a good future with IBM. But then he and his wife were killed in an automobile accident. Thank God Sara survived and I raised her here, with Jake helping."

She broke down in tears again.

Ken had been trying to follow all of this, his eyes flicking between the participants.

"Martha, let me get this straight. Sara wrote the

novel based on your experiences. You are the Jan in the novel and you guys hatched this up to expose the conspiracy around JFK's death?

"That's what I told Sara, but there's more, Ken. I gave Sara the information to base her novel on so we could smoke out the bastard who killed David, my son's father, and Sara's grandfather. But I had no idea he was still alive and had actually organized the assassination."

"And you were the sniper on the knoll?"

"You got it, Tierney. I was supposed to be the second patsy, but unlike Lee I escaped both the feds and the mob."

"So you killed JFK?"

"That's a bit blunt, wouldn't you say?"

"So my dad's theory was right after all…"

"Not quite, but that can come later. First I have some unfinished business." Before Ken realized what she was about to do, she pulled the trigger and hit the Don in the other leg. He writhed and howled in pain while she smiled.

"What about Chicago and Tampa? You would have set us up to be the patsies then if the assassination had worked, wouldn't you? How were you going to do it?"

"No, no, we…"

Martha worked the bolt again.

"No. Don't fire…I'll tell you. In Chicago Johnny would just have driven away after you and Lee fired. In Chicago it was to be like it worked in Dallas. Johnny would abandon you up in the building, probably by knocking you out, and Lee would not have had enough time to escape from the tower he was firing from."

"Okay," said Martha. "And now you're going to

tell me who killed Bobby Smith."

"Who?"

Martha fired into the blacktop alongside David's head.

"Okay, okay. We were watching him and your father. We knew your sister had a child, but we obviously didn't know he was yours. When Rob, Bobby that is, booked his flight to Europe we figured he was coming to meet you. And it worked. Unfortunately he got in the way and Tony got too enthusiastic."

"Did you ever realize that Bobby had no idea where I was? It was just a horrible coincidence?" Martha kicked him on the leg. He shrieked with pain. "I had two chances at a decent family life and you killed both of them."

"Jan...please..."

"My name is Martha! So whose finger was it that you sent me all nicely wrapped in cotton wool?"

Before David could answer, Martha fired again, hitting his hand.

He screamed. "No...no more...please."

"Answer the question."

"Jan... Martha... please."

"Whose fingers?" She worked the action again.

"He was a nobody. He'd sold us out to another mob. He deserved it."

"Did you kill him afterwards?"

His face contorted in pain. "Me personally? No. Tony did it."

"On your orders?"

He gulped. "Yes."

"Where is Tony now?"

David just grimaced.

Ken kicked the nearest goon lying on the road. "You're Mike, right? What happened to Tony?"

David shouted, "Don't say a word."

Mike stayed silent until Ken kicked him again and said, "You or him."

"The Boss killed him. He thought that Tony was getting too ambitious."

Martha looked down at David. "So what happened to Johnny and Marv? I heard that Johnny was killed. Was it you that shot him and dumped him in the bay in that oil drum?"

"I don't know what you're talking about. What oil drum? And why would I want to get rid of Johnny?"

"You did, didn't you? I can see it in your eyes. He was a loose end, just like me." Martha jerked the barrel of the rifle in his direction. "What about Marv?"

"He always said it would be his last job and took his money and ran. I never heard from him again."

"And Jack Ruby? How did you get him to kill Lee?"

"Jack liked the idea of going out with a bang. He was broke and his strip clubs were losing money he didn't have. We offered him a way out and he had nothing to lose. It was too dangerous to have Lee in jail. He knew too much and who knows what kind of deals he'd get offered. Jack was low risk. So he did us all a favor and made himself a huge reputation."

"So you put him in jail where he died of cancer. And did you have a plan to get rid of me too? Or did you just hope that I'd get shot by the cops on the knoll as Tony and Johnny got away?"

The Woman on the Knoll

"Jan...I..."

"My name is Martha! The Jan that you knew back in 1963 is dead. Because of you. Do you know that after the assassination I even tasted the blood in that Dallas apartment thinking it was yours. You ruined my life." She looked down on David. "You've ruined too many lives, David. Even though you're Sara's grandfather and I loved you all my life until today..."

David knew what was coming next and his eyes widened in fear. A fear that eclipsed the pain he was feeling. Martha fired and put another round in his chest. His howling stopped.

The three guys stretched out on the road had their heads raised. Their faces were a picture of anguish. Martha raised her rifle and looked toward them. "You guys can get lost. You never were here, and neither were we. In 1963 your boss made a huge mistake but you weren't with him then. Just remember who is saving your lives now. Pick up these three pieces of filth, load them in the truck and get out of here."

They 'got'.

Martha said, "Dammit, I'm going to have to move again, Sara. Never know when they might come back." Then she went across to Jake's body and wept.

Sara just stood there, in shock.

Ken couldn't believe all he'd heard. But what David and Martha had said seemed to explain everything. Holy Shit!

Sara was comforting Martha when he got to Jake's body.

Martha said quietly, "I told you it would work, darling, but to find the betraying bastard still alive, even if he was my fiance and your grandfather, I just couldn't let him live." Then Martha smiled, went rigid, her eyes closed, and she collapsed.

The Woman on the Knoll

Fifty-three

Ken stood alongside Sara and watched as Martha's casket was lowered into the grave. He felt Sara shake and put his arm through hers. Gray drizzle fell on them and the straps round the coffin squeaked as they were pulled clear. Sara kept a hold on his arm as she poured a handful of dirt on the coffin and Ken felt her shudder again. They stayed there for a minute, heads bowed, remembering the game old lady who'd had so much drama in her life.

Sara looked up at Ken. "Grandma would have loved this rain," she said. "The ultimate cliche, a wet and gray funeral. She was always telling me to put more narrative and description in my books." She paused, "And Jake would be pleased to be buried next to her. They were very close. He was the best friend she had and the first person to meet us when we moved here thirty years ago. Did I tell you that story?"

"Not yet," said Ken, smiling.

"Our old car stalled outside of town and Jake's was the only tow truck available. He was a long time getting out to us and Grandma gave him what for. They cussed each other out and then they were the best of friends, till last week." Sara's eyes filled with tears. "She deserved better than this. She lived in such fear and spent almost her whole adult life hiding."

As she was speaking Ken realized that the Kennedy assassinations had consumed him for too long. "And I've spent too much of mine hunting for conspiracies. Someone else can go after the truth about Bobby."

Sara pulled back from the edge of the grave and said, "I'd like to be alone for a while, Ken. You go talk to Anji and Nicholas."

"You sure?"

"Positive. I just need a walk with my thoughts."

"Okay."

Anji looked good in black, and her scarf hid the last few scars from her glass cuts. Nicholas still had his arm in a sling but Ken was still astounded that they had survived the fire. He hadn't thought it possible for anyone to get out of that inferno. Sara had been sure it was arson, but the investigators had ruled that out, finding evidence of an electrical short. Sara still wasn't convinced.

They smiled as he walked toward them during the general move away from the graveside. The rest of the mourners headed for their cars.

The three of them watched Sara as she wandered through the cemetery, head bowed.

"Is she okay?" Anji asked Ken.

"I think she will be, given time. We'll just leave her for a while. Martha led a hell of a life but Sara was with her for the calmer period, up till the last day or two."

Anji said, "Ken, I've known Sara for ten years and it never occurred to me that her Grandma had such secrets."

"Nor did Sara for a long time. I can't imagine how

she felt when Martha first told her."

"And I couldn't believe her novel when I read the first few chapters," Nicholas said. "I thought was too incredible, but now we'll be able to publish an even better book. We're holding the auction next week and three major houses want to bid on it."

"I know she's sorry for the way she treated you, Nicholas," said Anji. "I never thought she'd speak to you or me again."

Sara came back and joined their small circle. "I've decided how to finish the book," she said. "It'll be a great ending."

She leaned across and kissed Ken.

He kissed her back with an intensity he hadn't realized existed.

Fifty-four

Three days later Ken and Sara returned to the wreck of the cabin, all charred wood, twisted metal and melted glass.

"Just as well it burned down," Sara said. "We could never have explained how a truck demolished the front and it got all shot up."

"Do you think the police believed us?" said Ken.

"Two accidental killings and Martha dying of a heart attack when she saw her old friend Jake dead? I think so." Sara pointed at the concrete foundation where the kitchen used to be and said, "Come on, over here."

Burned roof beams had collapsed and the smell of wet charred wood rose around them as they climbed through the wreckage.

"It's probably under here," she said.

"What is?"

"The gun cabinet. It wasn't just for security; it was fire-safe too. There's something inside that you need to see."

Ken helped her push charred beams out of the way and ten minutes later they pulled the metal cabinet free of the debris.

The Woman on the Knoll

"I can tell you the rest of the story now," she said. "Everything in my novel is just as Martha said it happened. Even her expecting the FBI to turn up just before the assassination. She was expecting them because she had called and warned them two days before. She figured that then Tony couldn't blame her for the plot failing and so David would get released unharmed. She never understood why the feds didn't act on it."

"She wasn't the only one who called. There were quite a few anonymous tips," said Ken, "but the FBI and the CIA had a track record of disregarding what they thought were flaky calls and not passing the information on to the Secret Service.

"So she was waiting for nothing?"

"I'm afraid so."

Sara went quiet and tears ran down her cheeks.

Ken had one important question that he'd not yet asked. "Okay Sara, I can understand that Martha had to fire to show good faith to get David released. So did she shoot Kennedy?"

"Yes, she fired, with the old rifle you were so disparaging about. It's quite accurate even after all these years. But she didn't hit JFK; she aimed off and fired a shot that hit the curb. There's no way she would have shot at Kennedy, but I can't prove it."

"It's a Winchester, right?"

"You know it is, you helped me bury it in the..."

"Let's not say where it is, Sara."

"You think we're being watched?"

"I don't know, but if I were the FBI I would still have doubts about our account of the last few days."

"Well I thought we were quite believable. I think

they bought the murder story, especially after we killed that deer and spread its blood all over the stains on the road. They knew Jake well enough to know that he'd have challenged a hunter who shot a deer out of season." She went quiet as she thought back over the last week, then shook off the feelings. "Now help me get the cabinet into the car."

Back in their motel room, they dumped the safe in the tub and cleaned it off. Sara used a knife to dig the plug of ash out of the lock and after a few minutes struggle managed to unlock and open the door. Ken saw the empty slots from where they'd removed the rifle and pistol.

"So?" Ken said. "What's the big deal?"

"Remember I wouldn't let you open the drawer at the bottom?"

He looked at her. "Yeah...?"

"Open it now."

Ken yanked the handle. The metal creaked then the drawer squealed open.

"Pull it all the way out," she said.

"There's only an old cardboard box inside."

"Pick it up."

Ken lifted it and took it to the table in the bedroom where there was more light. The box was three by three inches, about two inches tall. Old printing on the sides and top had faded. He pulled at the cardboard lid, which crumbled. He blew the fragments away and saw dull brass cartridges neatly arranged, each in a cardboard separator. One cartridge space was empty.

"Why do you think only one is missing?"

He looked at it, her meaning sinking in. "Oh no...you're joking, right?"

The Woman on the Knoll

"No, I'm not."

"So the bullet that's not there is the one that..." Ken's voice tailed away.

"Let me back up. Martha told me what I thought was the whole story about a year ago. She had decided that now she was getting older that she wanted to let the world what really happened, but she realized that she'd just be seen as another crackpot. No one would take her seriously, so she convinced me we could use a novel to flush out the truth. But as we discovered last week, what she really wanted was to find out who killed David and to get revenge. I guess she didn't want to tell me that part. As you saw, her plan worked, except that she had no idea he was still alive."

"So the missing bullet from here is…"

"The one she shot at Kennedy. But she aimed to miss and hit the curb instead. Johnny fired the head shot from the knoll that killed JFK from the front. David had set her and Lee Harvey Oswald up to get caught while the real shooters escaped. Grandma was supposed to be the second patsy, to be caught while Johnny got away, but they didn't know that she'd thought out an alternate escape plan using the stroller. She just walked away with the rifle hidden in the scabbard. She'd only taken out one cartridge to fire and the rest were in the box hidden under the baby doll. She stashed the rifle and the ammo, she never told me where, and recovered them years later. I can't prove her story, but I don't believe that she hit Kennedy."

Ken smiled.

"Why are you...?"

"How would you like to be sure of that?" Ken said.

Her eyes opened wide. "Of what? That she didn't

hit him? How?"

"The shot she fired that hit the curb would have left residue on the concrete, right?"

"Well yeah, but the FBI took the curbstone away during their investigation. I read about it."

"Yes they did. But the shooting was in November 1963 and the FBI only removed the curb in April of 1964. Remember I told you about Dad going to all the scenes in Dallas? He took photos, he interviewed eye-witnesses, and he looked for physical evidence. He'd read that a bystander had been hit by a fragment from the curb and he found the smear where the bullet had impacted. He also saw that someone, presumably the Dallas police or the FBI, had scraped some of the lead away. He thought that if they'd done that and left the curb stone, then they weren't interested in it anymore, so he took some scrapings too."

"So what has this...?"

"Let me finish. Dad did a lot of research on this. Most bullets from a manufacturer's lot are consistent in composition. But Mannlicher, who made the rifle that Oswald shot, used a lot of recycled lead in their bullets, old bullets, car batteries etc. so no one could ever prove whether the smear was from his shot or not because the bullet composition varied so much. Winchester though, they used much better grade lead, with specific impurities added to harden the bullet."

"Whoa...are you saying that we could analyze the lead in other bullets in the box and check for a match with the scrapings?"

Ken smiled. "You got it. I still have all of dad's evidence. If there is a match it wouldn't prove in a court of law that Martha hit it directly; it could possibly have been a ricochet after hitting something, or someone, else, but as far as I'm concerned, it would clinch that she was telling the truth."

"Let's do it. How long would it take? Who could do it? Where can we…?"

Ken held up a hand. "Give me two cartridges and we'll know in a week."

"A week? Why so much time?"

"Sara, trust me; I know how long the tests can take. Between us dad and I worked on this for over 50 years, we can wait a week.

THE END

Duncan King

This is a work of fiction. It is loosely based on historical events but I have taken literary license with some elements of time and space. The most blatant of these distortions are the locations of the bullet-chipped curbstone on Elm Street and of the sewer system around Dealey Plaza. There are also other deviations from official records and unofficial accounts, but no prizes for identifying them. Please remember this is a novel.

Printed in Great Britain
by Amazon.co.uk, Ltd.,
Marston Gate.